P9-DBR-310

Carolina Dream

Connie Squiers

WestBow
P R E S S®
A DIVISION OF THOMAS NELSON
& ZONDERVAN

Copyright © 2019 Connie Squiers.

All rights reserved. No part of this book may be used or reproduced by any means, graphic, electronic, or mechanical, including photocopying, recording, taping or by any information storage retrieval system without the written permission of the author except in the case of brief quotations embodied in critical articles and reviews.

WestBow Press books may be ordered through booksellers or by contacting:

WestBow Press
A Division of Thomas Nelson & Zondervan
1663 Liberty Drive
Bloomington, IN 47403
www.westbowpress.com
1 (866) 928-1240

Because of the dynamic nature of the Internet, any web addresses or links contained in this book may have changed since publication and may no longer be valid. The views expressed in this work are solely those of the author and do not necessarily reflect the views of the publisher, and the publisher hereby disclaims any responsibility for them.

Athena McKinzie, of Fine Art America, took the beautiful cover photograph and this Friesian stallion's name is Encore.

ISBN: 978-1-9736-5546-6 (sc)
ISBN: 978-1-9736-5545-9 (hc)
ISBN: 978-1-9736-5547-3 (e)

Library of Congress Control Number: 2019902552

Print information available on the last page.

WestBow Press rev. date: 4/30/2019

Carolina Dream

Contents

Chapter 1

———— ❦ ————

The Letter

"**M**ackenzie, will you please be a sweetheart and go out and get the mail. I'm busy fixing lunch, and I know you're hungry."

She answered "Yes, Papa, as she passed through their small kitchen." Minutes later she came in with a big stack and dumped it on the kitchen table. "It seems we get more mail every day."

He shook his head as he sliced a big tomato, "It's a shame someone has to die before friends will send cards or write. In the old days ..."

"I know, I know, Papa, people used to write letters to each other before we had email."

He laughed, "You always seem to know what I'm going to say."

"That's because you say the same thing every time I bring in the mail."

He smiled and shook his head, "Yes, I guess I do." He looked over at the stack of mail, washed and dried his hands, then sat down at the table. "Let's see who has blessed us with cards today."

He slowly shuffled through the stack, smiling when he found a letter from someone they hadn't heard from in a long time. Suddenly, he stopped and examined a letter more closely. *This can't be. This one's from my papa. I haven't spoken to him for almost fifteen years.*

Mackenzie noticed a strange look on her father's face, "What's the matter Papa."

He looked up and smiled, "It's nothing, Sweetheart. It's just a letter from your grandfather."

She snorted, "From the one I've never talked to or met?"

"Now Mackenzie, that's no way to talk. He was nice enough to send us a letter."

"Papa, you never told me why you and your family are not close, or why you left Spain."

He looked sad, "It's a tragic story, my little one, but one I probably need to tell you. After I finish fixing your lunch we can go sit on the porch and talk."

She stomped her foot, "No! I want to hear it now. You always told me you left Spain because you wanted to find a job in America, but I know that's not the whole story, and it's something I've always wanted to know."

He wiped his hands on a dish towel and asked her to sit down. "Mackenzie, I told you our love story, and it was the truth, because I would never lie to you. As you know, your mother and I met on a beautiful sunny day, at a horse show in

Spain." He smiled, "We fell in love, and stayed in love, because of our love for horses. I wanted to come to America and work at a big horse farm, so I answered ads in the paper. Finally, one showed an interest. I guess they liked that I'd been raised around horses on a very well-known horse farm near Granada, Spain. They figured I had the experience they needed, so they offered me a job right here on Sunrise Farm ... the farm where we live now."

"Papa, I know all this. Tell me something I *don't* know." Then she thought of another question, "By the way, why did you take a job at a farm in Camden, South Carolina? There are others you might have chosen."

"To tell you the truth, Mac, it was the only one that answered my application. The others ignored it. So, I guess you can say it was God that led us here, and I've not regretted it for a second."

She smiled and nodded, "Now, tell me the rest of the story ... the part I don't know."

He frowned, but had laughter in his eyes, "Be patient Mackenzie, I'm getting to it." He took a sip of water then continued, "As I've said many times before, your mom and I fell in love in Spain, and we were married there. What you don't know is my parents disliked your mother intensely. In fact, they hated her."

His daughter was shocked, "Why? She was the nicest person I've ever known. How could they hate her?"

"They didn't like your mother because she was not Catholic. Back then, Catholics could not marry anyone who was not Catholic, because they'd be ex-communicated if they did.

3

Ex-communicated means they would be thrown out of the church. My parents were very old-fashioned, and thought it was the worst thing that could ever happen to a family. They thought marrying outside the Catholic church meant their son or daughter would go to hell when they died."

"Wow, that's pretty drastic. So, you left because they didn't like Mom?"

"I left because they told me they didn't want to ever see me again ... that I was dead to them because of what I had done."

Mackenzie was alarmed, "Papa, how could they do that? They were your parents! They were supposed to love you no matter what!"

He returned his attention to the letter, "Since this letter is in Spanish, I'll translate it for you as I read. My father started out with 'Dear Son', which surprised me since he'd basically disowned me." He continued reading, "I know you write to your brother, Angelo, and he told me your wife died recently. I offer you my prayers, and have been lighting candles, in hopes you find peace with your loss. Your mother died two years ago, so I know how you must feel. My biggest regret in life is that I never contacted you, and never got to meet my granddaughter, but I know her name is Mackenzie. Angelo showed me pictures of her each time you sent them, and she's beautiful. Give her a hug from me, and tell her I have loved her in my heart since the time she was first born. She's my only grandchild. I am very sick and will not be around much longer, but I want to give you a gift, in hopes you'll forgive this old man his stupid, stubborn ways." Miguel read further, but silently, *Don't read this part to your daughter, but I am sending you something I love, in hopes you will think of me sometimes. Your gift will arrive in about two weeks ... and bring a horse trailer with you when you go to pick it up. You'll get another letter from me when it is delivered.* Her dad started reading aloud again, "I'm thinking of you. *Te amo tanto mucho, Su padre.*"

"Papa, what does the Spanish part mean?"

He looked over at her with tears in his eyes, "It means I love you very much. Your father."

All she said was "Awwwwwww, how sweet," then added, "It's about time he told you he loved you." Then she asked, "What do you think he's sending you?"

"Whatever it is Mac, I'll treasure it, because it'll be from my papa."

"How can you forgive him for driving you and Mom from their lives?"

"God tells us to forgive and helps us do it. It hurt a lot when it first happened, but the pain gradually went away when we had you, and a wonderful life here with the horses. Now, I just feel bad that he missed out on loving you, and seeing you grow up. So, the loss is really his."

She remarked hotly, "What about me? I lost out, too. I never even got to meet him!"

"Punkin, your loss is part of the tragedy, because he loved horses like we do, and you would've been crazy about him. But yes, your loss was terrible as well, because you never got to know each other."

"Why does God tell us to forgive people who hurt us like that? It's not what we feel like doing."

"When we forgive someone, we're being obedient to what

the Bible tells us to do. God knows forgiving someone helps us to release anger we sometimes hold inside, because it frees us up to focus on other things, like loving each other, and our precious horses."

Chapter 2

———⟨⦿⟩———

The Wonderful Gift

Knowing a gift was coming from her grandfather was driving Mackenzie crazy, which meant she was driving her father crazy. "Papa, what on earth could take so long to get from Spain to South Carolina? If you know what it is, tell me. Why won't you tell me, I'm your daughter? Will I like it? Don't be so mean. I want to know." Her dad told her he should have known better than to tell her anything about the gift because he knew she would keep pestering him to tell her what it was.

Two weeks later they got a call requesting they pick up a large shipment at the Charleston Port Authority. Mackenzie wondered what kind of gift would take two weeks to get from Spain to South Carolina. She was even more perplexed when her dad hitched a horse trailer to his truck. She commented, "It must be a pretty big gift to need a trailer to haul it home." Her dad smiled, but said nothing.

Two hours later they arrived at the Charleston port and a guard directed them to the live freight section. Mackenzie looked around, wondering why the gift would come by ship. Suddenly, a door opened and a dock worker led a beautiful light grey mare to where they were standing, then he carefully read from the document in his hand. "Are you Miguel Perez? If so, please sign this invoice to certify your shipment was delivered."

Her dad answered yes, then signed without taking his eyes off the horse. He was accustomed to seeing beautiful horses on Sunrise Farm, but this one took his breath away. She was gorgeous. He was then handed a thick envelope, which he quickly opened and started reading. It was another letter from his father. This time he read it out loud, "Miguel, I want to introduce you to *Sueño Ibérico*, or as you would say, Iberian Dream. Her papers are in order and included in this envelope. I've also taken the liberty of enclosing documents certifying this beautiful mare was bred to my best stud, *Sueño de Plata*, which, as you know, means Silver Dream. She is due to foal next April. My wish is that Mackenzie be given this foal from her grandfather, with his love, and that you two may ride these horses together for many years to come." Tear flowed down her father's cheeks as he read. Hearing from his dad was emotional, but he continued reading to his daughter.

Mackenzie's eyes opened wide when the letter said the mare was to have a foal, and when it was born it was to be given to her. She started crying as well. She couldn't believe she would soon have a horse of her own! She'd always been able to ride some of the horses at Sunrise, but this was different. This would be her *own* horse ... for her to love, train, and ride. Her tears came so fast she started hiccupping, making the mare toss her head and quickly back up. This made her started laughing, and her dad smile.

When they got home, Dream was led to a freshly cleaned stall, where she nibbled the hay, then began loudly sucking water from her bucket. She was thirsty from her long trip.

Her dad made sure all the other horses at Sunrise were comfortable and taken care of, but he kept checking on the mare, still not believing she was here and his.

The next day Mackenzie and her dad took Dream out of her stall to get a better look at her. She was a beautiful dappled grey. The filly pranced as he led her around the paddock, her long mane and tail shimmering in the sunlight.

When he finally saddled her, he rode out to the pasture where Dream could stretch her legs after the long trip. He was surprised when the grooms at Sunrise left the stables to watch. They clapped and whistled as he put her through her paces. It made him proud of his horse, but worried him because he didn't want his boss thinking he was trying to draw attention away from the Sunrise horses.

After their short ride, he took Dream back to her stall. While brushing her he muttered under his breath, "Thoroughbreds are bred to go fast, and my horse was not. They aren't in competition with each other at all."

The next day Sunrise's owner, Martin Collins stopped by to see the new addition, and they talked. "Miguel, so this is the horse your father said he was sending? She's not a Thoroughbred, like most of the horses here, but she's a beauty. Didn't you say her name is Iberian Dream."

"Yes sir. She's an Andalusian, and more beautiful than I expected. She also has a P.R.E. before her registered name, which stands for *Pura Raza Espanola*. That certifies she's a horse of the Pure Spanish Breed. It may not mean much here in the United States where there aren't many Andalusians, but it does in Spain, and to the Andalusian horse community around the world."

"So, it's true, your dad is a big time horse breeder in Spain? I know you're good with horses, but I wondered if what your application for employment said was true."

"Yes sir, but not a breeder like you, Mr. Collins. I know raising Thoroughbreds is a *really* big deal here in the States," which made his boss smile.

He patted Miguel on the back, "Glad we have room for her with us. That might change in the future, but for now she's very welcome."

Miguel was pleased to get compliments on his new mare, but a little uneasy when Mr. Collins implied they might not always have room for Dream at Sunrise Farms. When he got home, he was careful not to share his concerns with Mackenzie because it would worry her.

Chapter 3

———◦✦◦———

Iberian Dream

For several days, he thought about what Mr. Collins had said, and it made him think he may need to reconsider having his own farm. He and his wife had always put away money, in case they wanted to start that farm, and it looked like he might need to buy a place to keep Dream and her foal. As he drove around Camden, he noticed things about the town he hadn't paid much attention to before. He'd been too busy at Sunrise to really see it through the eyes of a newcomer.

He already knew Camden was a heavily wooded and peaceful small town in South Carolina. He tried to recall what else he knew about it. It was located about 29 miles north of Sumter, and 30 miles northeast of Columbia, the state capitol. He was well aware of these distances, because he often had to travel with the Sunrise horses to different race tracks up and down the East Coast. There was no doubt the horse industry was a major part of this little town's economy. When he looked to his right, he noticed a sign claiming Kershaw County to be the *Steeplechase Capital of the World*, not to mention it was home to *The Carolina Cup* and *The National Steeplechase Museum*. He'd been so busy with the horses, he hadn't really seen much of what the small town had to offer.

He knew many owners from the Eastern part of the U.S., and really throughout the world, and many sent their horses to Camden to train at their facility. No wonder he'd always been so busy. He hadn't minded though, because he'd gotten to meet many of the Hall of Fame trainers who sent their horses to Camden for a winter rest, or rehab following an injury.

He took a detour and drove by the steeplechase museum's entrance and paused a moment to look at the life-size bronze statue of 'Lonesome Glory'. That horse had been a record-setting, five-time Horse of the Year winner. He loved living here because Camden was steeped in racing tradition and he was proud of its history.

Mac found her dad with Dream when she came home from school, and saw him still brushing the horse's already sparkling coat. She stroked the mare's silken neck, then offered her some peppermint candy, because she knew most of the horses at Sunrise loved them.

While still brushing the mare, he asked, "How was school today?"

She laughed, "I hardly knew what the teacher was saying, because I was thinking about Dream."

He scolded her, "You can't let your mind wander because you need to know what they are teaching you."

"I know, Papa. I'll do better tomorrow. How's our Dream today."

He responded, "She great ... and more than I thought she might be. Tomorrow is Saturday and you can ride her then ... unless you don't want to."

She laughed, "Stop teasing me, of course I want to. And Papa, after dinner I'm going to read to you. It'll be parts of a book I checked out from the school library and it's on the Andalusian breed." He smiled and she knew he wanted her to share what she had learned, even though he already knew all about the horses.

That evening after dinner they didn't turn on the television, but settled down in the living room so Mackenzie could read to him. She cleared her throat and started, "The Andalusian, also known as the Pure Spanish Horse or PRE (*Pura Raza Española*), is a horse breed from the Iberian Peninsula, where its ancestors have lived for thousands of years. The Andalusian has been recognized as an individual breed since the 15th century, and its conformation has changed very little over the centuries. For many years it was known as a great war horse and was prized by the nobility. The Spanish government often gave these Spanish horses to kings across Europe." Her dad interrupted, "Why do you think they gave those horses away?"

Mackenzie thought a minute, "I guess as a peace offering." He nodded and had her continue. "The Andalusians came here when the Conquistadors came to America. These horses left their mark on our wild Mustangs, some of which still bear the Spanish look, such as does the much sought-after Kiger Mustangs of Oregon. Exports of Andalusians from Spain were restricted until the 1960s, but since then, the breed has spread throughout the world. In 2010, there were more than 185,000 registered Andalusians worldwide. These horses are strongly built, and compact yet elegant. They have long, thick manes and tails, and their most common coat color is gray, but they can be found in many other colors." She paused and looked at her dad, "We know that, don't we Papa?"

He nodded and motioned for her to continue, "They are known for their intelligence, sensitivity and willingness to please. Over the years, the Andalusian breed has been selected for its athleticism and stamina. The horses were originally used for classic dressage, driving, bullfighting, and as stock horses. Modern Andalusians are used for many equestrian activities, including dressage, show jumping, and driving."

She stopped to ask her dad a question, "Did you know Andalusians are used a lot in movies, like historical pictures and fantasy shows?"

He smiled, "Mackenzie, do you really think I don't keep track of the breed? They are my favorite horses and I was raised loving them, so of course I know how they are used here in America and around the world. I think they are the best of all the breeds."

"You like them more than Mr. Collins' horses?"

"As I told you before, they each have their strong points, but overall, I'll take the Andalusians any day." She smiled as she put the book down, then came over to give him a hug. "Me, too, Papa." She changed the subject, "So when will Dream have her foal?"

He responded, "Papa's letter mentioned she was bred in May of this year, so she'll foal next April sometime. Perhaps she'll deliver on your birthday!" Mackenzie grinned, "I'd like that."

Chapter 4

—◦◦◦—

Unrest at Sunrise

Mackenzie loved riding Iberian Dream and did so as often as possible. Mr. Collins was watching her and the horse, but also noticed the growing number of his clients stopping by to watch. Some even asked him questions about the new addition to his stable.

He would say, "Oh, that is my farm manager's horse."

One asked, "Can that filly run?"

The question jolted the farm's owner, "No, it's not a breed that can run. I believe it is called an Andy something?"

"Do you mean she's an Andalusian?"

He responded, "That may be the breed, but she's not built to run like our Thoroughbreds."

The man was curious, "But I understand they can jump. Have you ever seen her jump?"

"To tell you the truth, I really don't pay attention to any horses but Thoroughbreds."

The man glanced back at the horse and rider, then went to check on his horses. Immediately, Mr. Collins headed back to his office to check out what those horses could do. He couldn't have any of his Steeplechase clients looking at the horse. On Google, he typed in Ando and horse, because he couldn't remember how to pronounce or spell the name. Immediately, the server suggested Andalusian. He clicked on it, growing more nervous as he read about the horse, and some of the Andalusian jumpers that had competed in steeplechases, and even in the Olympics. He would have to do something about that horse. Hopefully, he hadn't invited a fox into his hen house. What if some clients became impressed with the breed and bought fewer of his Thoroughbreds?

Mr. Collins liked having Miguel as Sunrise's manager. He knew the man was constantly checking on the horses, and anyone who had contact with them, so he had to figure out a way to gently tell him they needed the stall he was using for more of their client's horses. He knew he couldn't afford to have him get mad and work somewhere else. Miguel was a very valuable asset, and the horse owners liked bringing their horses to the farm because him. They knew he was honest, hardworking, and talented. Above all, they knew he loved their animals. He thought, *what if they wanted to follow him to another farm?*

Mr. Collins struggled with how to handle moving the Andalusian away from Sunrise. What would Miguel say? When he'd promoted him to manager, part of the deal was he could have the use of one stall for his own private use. He really didn't want to wait until the foal they were expecting grew large enough to need an additional stall, because then they would need two. By then, some owners might want to replace some of their Thoroughbred jumpers with Andalusians. No, he would have to deal with the problem sooner than that.

The heat of the summer subsided and fall crept in slowly. South Carolina doesn't have a climate of extremes, except summer, which is hot and humid. It's autumns, winters, and springs, are generally mild and pleasant. As the months wore on, Dream started to show she was going to have a foal. Mackenzie still rode her, but the workouts were not long, nor difficult. She couldn't have anything happen to this precious horse. It was her foal's mama.

Mr. Collins still had not figured out how to approach Miguel about his horse. As the mare grew larger and more cumbersome, he knew he'd put off the unpleasant conversation long enough. It wouldn't be long before his Thoroughbred horse owners would want to trailer their mares in to give birth at the farm, especially if they intended to race their foals, or have them shown in futurities. Many had scheduled the births in early January or February, because for racing purposes, a Thoroughbred's official birthday is always listed as January 1st. Being born early in the year allowed for maximum growth during the racing season. It would be the perfect excuse.

In early November, Mr. Collins approached Miguel. First, he told him how he was valued at Sunrise, then explained he had a problem. More horses were coming in that needed stalls, so he would have to find somewhere else to put his mare.

Miguel was in shock. He'd expected to be told he had to leave, but he didn't have a place for Dream yet. He argued, "My employment contract clearly said I'd have a stall here for my private use. I have never used that privilege, but I need to do so now. What do you expect me to do?"

Mr. Collins shrugged, "I'm not sure what you're going to do, but I need the stalls. You know this is our busy time of year and it's critical to our operation that we have stalls available for everyone that wants one."

Miguel countered, "Except me. I need one. Dream is due to foal in the few months."

"Miguel, you know the horses coming in will be foaling soon. I believe yours is due sometime in April."

"Mr. Collins, you know this is a breach of my contract."

He shrugged, "I don't know what to tell you."

Miguel had been thinking this might happen and was prepared, "I'll settle for an extra five hundred dollars a month for the duration of my contact to overlook this breech."

The owner huffed, "That seems a little steep, Miguel. It won't cost you that much a month to board your horse somewhere else."

"I'm not putting her in a common stable. She'll need to go to a nice place, where she'll be comfortable and be treated well."

He thought for a minute, "Well, I guess I'll have to take your option as I really have no choice."

Miguel stuck out his hand, "So it's a deal. I'll drop by your office tomorrow to sign an agreement to that affect."

"I guess so. It'll take a day or two to get it drafted."

Miguel pressed him, "It is now the 2nd of November, I will

18

have until the end of November to find another place for my horse, correct."

Mr. Collins shook his hand and reluctantly agreed, but added, "You'll still be working here, won't you?"

"Yes sir, until my contract is up in June."

The owner panicked, "You *are* going to sign another contract with us, aren't you?"

"Sir, it depends ..." He left it at that, then turned to walk back to the stable.

Chapter 5

—◦◦◦—

Buying Miss Lillian's Horse Farm

The days seemed to fly by as Miguel looked for a suitable property with a stable already on the land. He found a few, but they were either too expensive, or too small. He was very frustrated as he pulled into his driveway.

Mackenzie ran out to meet him, "Did you find anything that would work for us?"

"Not yet, Sweetheart, but I'm hopeful."

"Papa, I was talking with Mrs. Sweeny at the grocery store today. You know, she's the older lady I often talk with who loves horses. I told her we were looking for a place. She said she was thinking about selling her property, but wanted to keep her three horses there. So far, no buyers considering her property, wanted to do that. They wanted her to clear out completely."

He was interested and asked, "Does her place have a house on it as well?"

"Oh yes, and it's quite nice. There's a cottage behind it and she thought she might like to live there instead of in the big house. She wants to stay near her horses. She said possible buyers were not happy with that either."

Her dad looked thoughtful, "I might give her a call and we can go over and see her. It might not be anything we'd like to buy, but then again, it might. At the very least, she might let us board Dream there for a while, until we find a suitable place."

The next day Mackenzie and her father drove over to see Mrs. Sweeny. Because they had called ahead to make sure she was home, she met them at the door with a plate of home-made cinnamon rolls. Miguel looked down at Mackenzie and whispered, "This is a great start." After they finished eating the treats she wanted to show them around the place. The house was fairly large, but a little shabby because she hadn't had anyone paint it.

"Mrs. Sweeny, can you show us the barn now. That's what we are really interested in." She moved slowly, but they eventually reached the stable where her horses were kept. Miguel was impressed, "Wow, someone really invested a lot of time and effort into putting this barn together. He reached over and touched a stall door frame. "What workmanship. You don't see this anymore. Everything now days seems to be thrown together in a hurry."

She said with pride, "My Henry built the interior of this barn himself. He was a master carpenter, you know. He told me he wanted our horses to have the best, so he made sure it was up to his high standards."

Miguel admired the craftmanship and commented, "It shows he cared." He looked at her and rubbed his chin, "I'm going to be honest with you, Mrs. Sweeny, we don't have a whole lot of money to put into a place, so please don't be offended if we don't offer you what it's worth."

"Young man, I want to sell my farm, but as I told your daughter, I want to stay in the cottage in the back, and use three of the stalls for my horses."

Miguel responded, "That's not a problem. I am the manager at Sunrise Farms and I like things maintained and neat, so I'd be working around here to fix anything in disrepair."

Mrs. Sweeny clapped her hands, "And would you take care of my horses as well?"

Mackenzie immediately assured her she would be glad to take care of the horses herself, because she loved doing it. She made a special effort to ask the horses' names, which pleased he old woman immensely.

Miguel turned to her, "I guess now we should discuss the price." He paused because he forgot to ask a question, "How many acres do you have here, Mrs. Sweeny?"

She scolded him, "Call me Lillian. My name is Lillian and we *have* become friends, haven't we?"

"Sure thing, Lillian."

"There are about a hundred and sixty acres here. My land extends quite a way beyond those trees."

Miguel was surprised it was so big, and asked another question, "And how many stalls do you have?"

"We have 30 stalls, two extra rooms, and a two-room shed out back to store the feed, and a large tack room. Oh, and another building to store hay. Henry didn't want to take a chance on a fire getting started in the hay and roaring through the stable. A fire would probably kill our precious horses."

Miguel was impressed, "It sounds like Henry knew what he was doing by laying the buildings out that way?"

She smiled, "My Henry did everything well."

"I can see that."

"We need to discuss price now, Mrs. Swe ... I mean Lillian."

"I'm eighty-two now and have no children to give this place to, so I could let you have it for three-hundred and fifty thousand dollars because you said I can stay here with my horses, and you would fix the place up for me."

Miguel was shocked the price was so low. He knew it was located only five miles from the racetrack, and seven miles from Sunrise, because he clocked it on his way to see her. He reached out his hand and said, "You've got a deal Mrs. Sweeny, and don't worry, we'll take care of you and those horses of yours."

She added, "Will your daughter exercise them for me sometimes?"

Mackenzie spoke up, "I'll be glad to do that, Miss Lillian."

Before they got in the truck to leave, Mrs. Sweeny put her hand on Miguel's arm, "One more thing. On the other side of those trees we have track, if you should need it. It's quite overgrown now, but it shouldn't take too much to get it in shape."

It was all he could do to keep a smile off his face. This place was beyond his wildest dreams, and was something he could afford. They waved good bye and told her they'd be by with sales contract the next day. She smiled and waved back.

Mackenzie and her dad rode in silence for a couple of minutes, then they both started talking at once. "Papa, God must be looking out for us."

"Amen, Mac. This is truly a blessing for us, but I think it will be for Lillian as well. She can remain on her own property, her horses will be taken care of, and we'll be around in case she needs us. She shouldn't be alone here at her age."

"Papa, can I adopt her as my grandma?"

He smiled over at here, "Absolutely, and I think she'd love to have a granddaughter. Being alone in the world with no relatives, especially no children, must be lonely."

Mackenzie grinned, "Maybe she'll make some more of those cinnamon rolls. They were yummy."

"And maybe we can cook for her sometimes. You've gotten pretty good in the kitchen since your mom died. I think this is going to work out great for all three of us."

Chapter 6

———ↄoↄ———

Moving On

A few days later Mr. Collins stopped Miguel near the barn, "You've been looking pretty happy lately, Miguel. I like to see my farm manager in a good mood. The trainers and grooms like to see it as well."

Miguel didn't tell him why he was always smiling, because he didn't want to be told to move Iberian Dream just yet. He still had a lot of work he wanted to do on the place before they moved in.

Mackenzie was still exercising Dream and more people stopped to look at the beautiful horse. Someone yelled to her, "Hey, Mackenzie, have you tried to jump that beast of yours yet?" She knew he was teasing her, because he was smiling, but it got her to thinking. Andalusians were used as show jumpers, maybe hers could jump as well. She debated whether to even try it since her horse was now pregnant, but decided taking a small jump wouldn't hurt anything. She rode her horse into a ring where some low jumps were already in place and patted her neck. "Now Dream, we'll just try a small one for now, because you've probably never jumped before." She lined her up and spurred her on to the first jump, which was very low. She smoothly sailed over it and started towards the next one. Mackenzie thought maybe they could try another. What would it hurt? Dream jumped that one as well. Instead of reining her in like she'd planned, she guided her to the next jump, then the next. The final one was almost three feet tall. She knew she should have stopped at one or two feet, but the mare seemed eager to jump more.

She didn't know it, but there were several owners and grooms watching her. Someone commented to those around him, "I understand Mackenzie hadn't jumped any of these before, but she and that horse of hers performed beautifully."

When she finished the course, she reined Dream in and reminded those watching that her horse was almost six months pregnant, then she headed back to their stall. A few horsemen came over as she was cooling Dream down. "Was your horse a jumper in Spain? She looked great out there."

Mackenzie responded, "Not that I know of. I've just been working her on dressage routines. My papa never said anything about her jumping. I probably shouldn't have tried it today because she is due to foal in five months, but I wanted to knew if she could jump as well.

Each of them approached the horse and ran their hands along her neck and flank, admiring her color and the silkiness of her coat. "What kind of horse did you say she is?"

"She's an Andalusian. She came from a very well-known horse farm in Spain."

They all commented, "She's a beauty," then walked away, talking among themselves.

Mr. Collins had also seen Dream jump the entire course, and had noticed the men following Mackenzie so they could speak with her. When they headed back to their own horses, he wondered what they were talking about, hoping they weren't comparing her horse to theirs. That would be bad for business ... *very* bad for business. He'd have to speak with Miguel very soon about moving the mare elsewhere. He wasn't sure where they could board her at a reasonable price, but she had to go ... the sooner the better.

After Miguel closed on the property, he spent every spare minute fixing it up. He knew for sure the house and outbuildings needed painting, and the barn cleaned out. It was obvious Lillian hadn't had help around there for a while, because even her horses' stalls needed mucking out, but he was glad to do it for her. She was such a pleasant person and the deal he received on the farm was unbelievable, and an answer to prayer.

As farm manger, he'd had a small house to live in at Sunrise, so when he moved his belongings out, Mr. Collins questioned him. "You must have found another place to stay, Miguel. Does it have room for your horse and the foal she's going to have?"

He turned and smiled, "It sure does Mr. Collins," but he said no more.

The next day he was asked, "So when are you taking your horse to the new place, and will you need to borrow a trailer to get her there?"

Miguel answered, "We thought we'd make the transfer this weekend, and no, I'll not need to use one of your trailers."

His boss was confused, "So where are you moving?"

He stopped and turned around, "Do you remember Henry Sweeny's old place? That's where we're going."

Mr. Collins was shocked, "So the Sweeny's are renting you a place to stay?"

He took a moment to respond, "No sir, we're buying the property."

"Buying the Sweeny place? Where are the Sweeny's going then?"

"Henry died a few years ago, and his wife, Lillian, is going to live in the cottage out back, so she can be near her horses." He added, "Mr. Collins, don't worry about us, we're going to get along fine at that farm."

He was not done asking questions, "That's a pretty big place, isn't it?"

"Yes, sir, it is ... and we're going to enjoy living there."

He continued asking questions, "They have a racetrack out back don't they?"

Miguel laughed, "They sure do. I've almost finished clearing it out. It was quite a mess."

Now Mr. Collins was really intrigued, "I don't mean to pry, but how are you going to afford that place? We pay you well here, but that's a large farm and close to the track."

Miguel turned to him, "Don't you worry about us, Mr. Collins. We'll be fine."

He started to ask another question, but Miguel held up his

hand, "I'm sorry, but I have a lot to do today, but nice talking with you."

Sunrise's owner was left thinking about what he'd just heard, and what it would mean for his business. Would horse owners want to board at Miguel's place instead of with him. He walked back to his office, shaking his head, and wishing he'd never mentioned having him take his horse elsewhere, because this could mean trouble.

Chapter 7

—⟨*⟨*⟩*⟩—

Dreamland is Named

When Miguel arrived home he walked in the house to the smell of pot roast and homemade chocolate chip cookies. Mackenzie looked up as she was taking the last few from the cookie sheet, "Look what Lillian taught me to make? I can hardly wait until dessert."

He walked over and hugged his daughter, "Smells great little one. Tonight at dinner we're going to think up a name for this beautiful horse farm, so be thinking about it."

At the table Mackenzie suggested *Rocking Horse Farm* or *Paradise Farm*. Lillian clapped with each suggestion. She'd never had a family, except Henry, and the banter back and forth thrilled her. Never in a million years had she even dreamed she would be part of a real family. She was happy and content.

"Mac, those are nice choices, but I've been giving this a lot of thought. How about something with the word Dream it in, like maybe *Dream Horse Farm?*"

Mackenzie interrupted, "How about *Dream Maker Farm?*

"Not bad, Mackenzie. Let's write down the suggestions, and think about them overnight. Maybe we can come up with a decision by tomorrow. It's got to be the perfect name. I want to have a sign made soon, so we can't put this off."

As they discussed the names the next evening, Lillian suggested another, "How about *Dreamland Farm*. If you start taking in other horses to train and board, you'd be helping owners fulfill their dreams."

The name clicked with all three, "That's a great name, Lillian. Let's go with that one." They all agreed, so it was settled.

Miguel knew a local sign maker, who was more than happy to put a rush on the job. A week later it was delivered and hung over the farm entrance. It was the first thing Mackenzie noticed when she came home from school. "Oh Papa, it's beautiful! I love it. I especially like the twisted vines he painted around the edges."

Her dad beamed with her approval. "Miss Lillian loved it, too. I don't think she ever thought she'd be a part of another horse farm ... and she is. We've grown to love her, and she has great ideas, like the name for our farm."

Mackenzie nodded and ran to the house, shouting, "Lillian, the sign is perfect, isn't it!"

Three days later a pickup truck drove slowly by the farm and saw the sign. Immediately, it punched the gas to get out of there. Sunrise Farm's owner was the person driving and he didn't like what he saw. Why would a person name a farm something like that if they weren't going to take in horses? Dreamland Farm sounded like they were opening for business as a competitor and he was not happy. When he returned to Sunrise he called for the farm manager to come to his office.

Miguel was checking feed inventory, but put down his tablet and made his way to Mr. Collins's office, wondering what the call could be about. The interruption could put him behind today, because he still had to meet with the groom and sort out their schedules for the new shipment of horses due in that afternoon.

He walked up the steps to the office and took off his hat, "What can I do for you Mr. Collins?" All he got was a cold stare. "Is there anything wrong that I have to take care of? I was just organizing the grooms since we are expecting more horses today."

"I drove by your place today and saw your new sign. What does Dreamland Farms mean? Are you trying to lure clients away from Sunrise?"

"No sir. I do want to take in horses and board them, but my goal has not been to steal your customers."

"Have you talked to anyone about this new enterprise of yours?"

"No sir, I don't believe I have. I did put an ad in the local paper trying to find people who want to board their horses." He smiled, "The *Thoroughbred Daily News* is a little rich for my blood. I know that's where Sunrise advertises."

"I don't like it Perez. I don't see how you can serve me well if you are running your own place. I want you out of here by the end of the month. That should give me enough time to find someone to take your place."

Miguel spoke, "But ..."

"No buts, Perez. You need to go. Hope you like the horse business. It's not as easy as you think."

Miguel was in shock, because he didn't know what he was going to tell Mackenzie. Without this job, they might have a difficult time making their mortgage payment, and would certainly not have money for repairs the farm needed.

When he sat down to eat, Mackenzie said, "Well?"

He knew exactly what she was asking, so he told her and Lillian what had happened.

The rest of the meal was very quiet. No one wanted to talk about the problem, but they were each trying to think of how they could bring in money.

The next night they all had suggestions; some were actually very good, and they discussed each one at length. "Papa, I can give riding lessons."

"Sweetheart, we only have four horses here, three are very old and haven't been ridden in quite a while, and the other is pregnant."

She made another suggestion, "We can board horses and give lessons to the kids who own them."

Her dad said that was a good idea, but first they had to find those kids.

Mackenzie was not discouraged, "I know what we can do! We can have a grand opening party for Dreamland Farm and invite some of the horse people you know. It would let people know we are open for business and they could see how nice our facility is ... plus, many people know you by your reputation."

He smiled at her, "Mac, that's a great idea, but we have a lot of work to do before this place sparkles in order to attract horse people. This is a small, but ritzy town and they expect a lot from their stable."

Mackenzie was excited, "So we can do it?"

Her dad's face fell, remembering how much work needed to be done, and how little money they had to make it happen, "Sweetheart, I don't know where we're going to get the money. Your mom and I saved a lot, but I put most of it in this place already. It was a great idea though."

Lillian cleared her throat, "I have a little money I can put toward the grand opening, and I'd be honored if you'd let help out."

Miguel looked at her like she was crazy, "Why would you do that, Lillian?"

She replied softly, "Because I love being here, and I don't want things to change unless they get better for you two. I can afford it, Miguel. I'm almost eighty-three, and will never spend all I have, so I might as well have the pleasure of seeing something good come of it."

He replied, "You know, we are talking serious money here if we do it right?"

She replied, "I know."

He smiled at her, "This makes me both uncomfortable and relieved. Your offer is a surprise. I don't really know how I feel about it, but it also gives me hope and would definitely take the financial pressure off me."

Mackenzie didn't say a word, but kept looking back and forth as they talked to each other. She'd been praying that there'd be a way out of this mess, and she truly believed this might be God's answer.

Chapter 8

—⟶ ৶৶ৡ ⟵—

Dream Big

The next day Miguel sat Lillian down and gratefully accepted her offer to help them.

At dinner she boldly asked, "Miguel, just what are your plans for this place? Do you want it to be a riding stable, a place to board horses, a place to train them, or a breeding farm?"

Now that he knew the farm would not fail for lack of funding, he needed to determine what their long-term goals would be. Up until now, he hadn't let himself dream big because he was afraid the farm would go broke. Now ... now he would have to really think about it. Did he want to get his name out in the community with the grand opening, and see what happens, or did he want to plan something bigger?

Lillian must have read his thoughts and interrupted, "Don't be afraid to dream big, Miguel. You have a responsibility to Mackenzie, and to these horses. I know your dad is very sick, but would you consider a trip back to Spain to see him? He might have some ideas for you. The money you'll have will pay for the trip."

Her comment startled him, because he'd been thinking about going back to Spain to visit his dad, but knew they couldn't afford it. Maybe now they could. He was the youngest of his dad's two sons, and knew his papa would be thrilled to see him, because it had been so long. Maybe he should check and see what that trip would cost.

That afternoon he called his dad and the housekeeper answered. In Spanish he asked, "I am Señor Perez's son from the United States. Is he available to speak with me, or has he passed away?"

She was excited when she heard his voice, "Miguel, is this really you? Your dad is not well, but he would be glad to speak with you. I'll take him the phone." Before she ran to tell his dad the good news she said, "This is Maria. Remember me? I was your nanny when you were just a little thing. I'm so glad to hear from you. It's been a long time ... too long. Just a minute and I'll get him on the phone." He could hear her steps as she ran down the hall.

Maria, he thought, *she's still there with dad. Amazing.*

Two minutes later his dad came on the line, "*Mi hijo* [my son], I am so pleased you called. I've been praying you would. How is your daughter, Mackenzie? I hope she's well. To what do I owe the pleasure of this call?"

"*Padre* [Father], I know you are very sick, but I wanted to call and invite myself for a visit. I need one of your wonderful hugs, as well as your advice." They talked until Miguel's father sounded exhausted, and apologized, saying he had to take his medication and a breathing treatment. Before he hung up, they worked out a day the next week for the visit. He would fly into Santiago and his dad's chauffer would pick him up at the airport and take him to their farm. When he put down the phone, he started praying with tears in his eyes, *Lord, thank you that my father is still alive and that I will be able to speak with him again. It's been so long since I've seen him. This meeting should have taken place years ago, but we were both too proud to call the other, to try and repair our relationship.* He wiped his eyes, *Father, you found a way. My papa is reaching out to me with open arms and I'm running towards him. It's a miracle that's been long overdue. I thank and praise you for this opportunity to see him before goes home to heaven and to you. Amen.*

Chapter 9

———∞∞———

Visit to Spain

The phone call started the healing, but a visit to Spain would finish it, because he would take Mackenzie to meet her *abuelo* ... her grandfather. She would love him, Maria, his old nanny, Angelo, his brother, and the horses. Above all, she had to meet the horses, because he knew she'd fall in love with them, too, just like she'd fallen in love with Iberian Dream.

Once they had boarded the plane, and had settled in their seats, her dad took a colorful brochure from his pocket, and spread it out on the tray table in front of them, "I want to tell you about where I lived so long ago."

She nodded for him to start, "My dad lives on a beautiful horse farm near Granada, Spain." He pointed to a map of Spain. "Granada is located at the foot of the Sierra Nevada Mountains." He pointed, "And as you can see it is where four rivers meet, so there is plenty of water around. In addition, the city is only about an hour away from the Mediterranean Sea. My father's ranch is named *Rancho Majestuoso,* which means the Majestic Ranch. He thought his horses were the absolute best, so he put a very elegant name on his place."

Mackenzie asked, "Were they the best horses?"

He smiled over at her, "They were splendid horses indeed, and yes, I thought they were the best. As we would tell people, 'Our horses are *magnifico,* or magnificent.'"

He continued with his history lesson, "In Spain, Andalusia was known as birth place of the Andalusian horse. They were strong, powerful, and greatly favored by Moorish kings." He paused, "I think you can tell by looking at Iberian Dream, Andalusians are beautiful, have those wonderful high stepping movements, and the traditional long manes and tails. On top of it all, they have a wonderful, trustworthy temperament."

"Papa, they sound perfect."

"Many people think they *are* the perfect horse. You'll see."

It had been an almost nine-hour flight, so Mackenzie had been able to sleep a few hours. Miguel could not sleep because he was too excited. He wondered what had changed in Granada since he'd moved away. Would there be many horses left in his father's stables? Would his dad be well enough to talk with him? He would soon find out.

Mackenzie was in awe of the mountains as they drove from Santiago towards Granada, "What a beautiful place to have been raised. South Carolina does not have these big mountains." She turned to him, "And you said there is an ocean nearby, didn't you?"

He smiled, "The Mediterranean Sea."

"Did you ever get to ride the horses in the water?"

Before he could answer, they got out of the car because Maria had come down the porch steps and was running toward the car with her arms open wide. First, she hugged Miguel, then she rushed to Mackenzie, *"Miguel, ella es hermosa!"*

He smiled, "Yes, Maria, she is beautiful. And, she could hardly wait to get here to see you, Papa, and the horses."

"So, there is another Perez who loves the horses? This is good. Your papa will be so glad to see both of you. He's been asking me the time every fifteen minutes, because he can no longer see his watch clearly."

Miguel was concerned, "Will he be able to see us? Are is eyes that bad?"

"No, but you may have to get close to him so he can get a good look."

Maria rushed off to tell him their guests had arrived. Five minutes later she brought him out in a wheel chair.

He greeted them in English, he said, "It's wonderful to see you, son. It's been too long."

"Yes, it has, Father." He gestured to his daughter, "And this, Papa, is your granddaughter, Mackenzie."

She stepped forward and offered him her hand, but he reached for her and pulled her into a big, warm hug. When he pushed her back so he could see her, he had tears in his eyes. "I've missed so much and I'm sorry, Mackenzie. Will you forgive this old man his silly ways?"

She nodded and said, "Of course, *Abuelo*."

"Ah, I see your father has been teaching you a little Spanish. I've been learning a little English. We should get along fine."

He turned and spoke to Miguel in rapid-fire Spanish. The only words she recognized were Andalusian and *caballo*, which meant horse. She hoped that meant they were going to look at the horses now, because she could hardly wait to see them. She knew what Iberian Dream looked like, but she wanted to see the father of the foal she would own shortly ... her foal.

Mackenzie looked around as they headed for the stables. She could see the beautiful mountains to her right and many white fences on her left, with horses in each pasture. Before they entered the stable, which was white with black shutters, she looked up to see the name *Rancho Majestuoso* emblazoned on a large sign above the door. The letters were gold on a background of black.

She asked in wonder, "Papa, you lived here when you were young?"

He smiled down at her, "Sure did, Mackenzie. It was like heaven to live in this place. Beautiful horses everywhere I looked."

She thought back to the reason he had to leave and it made her sad, until she heard whinnies coming from the barn. *That* sound always made her happy.

Mackenzie ran her fingers over the beautifully engraved nameplates attached to each stall. "Papa, what does this one say? I can't read Spanish."

"That one means Beautiful Dream."

"How about this one?"

"Black Dream."

She asked him several more, until he told her he couldn't read them all to her, but he *would* read the next one. "Meet the sire of the foal Dream will have in April. His name means Silver Dream."

"Oh Papa, he's the most beautiful horse I've ever seen. It looks like his mane probably shimmers in the sunlight."

"Sweetheart, let's find out. Would you like me to take him outside so you can see him better?"

Mackenzie was excited, "Oh yes! I'd love that."

Her father took the stallion by the halter, but the horse tossed his head trying to get away. He didn't want to go with someone he didn't know. Then Miguel spoke to him in Spanish and patted his velvety nose. "Come on, big boy. I have someone who wants to see what you look like." The stallion rushed out of the open stall, almost knocking Mackenzie down as he dragged her dad behind him. One jerk on the halter, and more soothing talk calmed him. He wasn't used to this man who was pulling him outside, but he *was* familiar with the Spanish he was now hearing.

Mackenzie was amazed at how well her dad controlled the stallion, but she shouldn't have been because he'd spent all his life handling and loving horses. When they reached the paddock, Silver Dream stood still, but was still snorting, and his eyes showed his distrust. Eventually, his fear became curiosity. He thought, *who is this stranger, and who is that little person beside him?*

With his free hand, Miguel slowly took a peppermint from his pocket and offered it to the still wary horse beside him. His words came lovingly in Spanish, *"Mi hermoso Sueño de Plata, no voy a hacerte daño. Quiero presentarles a mi hija, Mackenzie."*

"Papa, what did you say to him? He's eating the candy out of your hand."

He smiled, "I told him he was beautiful, that I would not hurt him, and I wanted to introduce him to my daughter." She smiled.

"Well Sweetheart, what do you think? Isn't he a beautiful sire for your foal?"

"Papa, he's *magnifico!*" She looked at him and smiled, "Is that how you say it in Spanish?"

He laughed, "It sure is, and he truly *is* magnificent."

She took a closer look at the beautiful stallion standing before her, "He's light gray, almost pure white, and his coat is so silky. I am *extremely* proud he's the father of Dream's foal."

"You should be." He looked back at Silver Dream, "This horse commands the highest Andalusian stud fee in all of *España*, which is Spanish for Spain. In the United States, you could buy an extremely nice house for what it would have cost me to breed our mare to a stallion of his quality."

She could only say, "I must thank your dad again for the wonderful gift, and I can hardly wait for our foal to be born."

"My brother, Angelo, will be here soon to ride him. I'm sure you'll want to stay and watch." She nodded.

Half an hour later Angelo arrived at the stable, introduced himself to Mackenzie, then went to get Silver's tack. After the horse was saddled, he mounted, then saluted them. "This beautiful horse is going to show off for you now." When he turned towards the center of the large paddock, they heard music playing in the background. He turned around in the saddle and explained, "Silver works better with music."

One of the grooms, who knew Silver was about to perform for the guests, raised the volume on the PA system so it could be heard loud and clear where they were doing their routine.

Mackenzie was blown away by Silver's performance. Angelo started with the passage, which was a measured, and very elevated trot. Her dad pointed at the horse, "Look Mackenzie. See how he's using the muscles in his hindquarters to push himself along, and see how he flexes his knees and hocks. He seems to float through the air in time to the music," Miguel looked down at his daughter, "Our Dream is very good at this, but Silver Dream is a master."

His attention returned to Angelo, "Ahh, the piaffe! Silver is good at this, too. Doesn't it look like he's trotting in place? His movements are light and airy, and his cadence is perfectly in time to the music."

Just then a groom ran out and called to Angelo, "Señor Perez, the caller you have been trying to reach is on the line." Miguel's brother dismounted, handed the groom the reins, then smiled, "Please excuse me Miguel, but I must take this call. You two must come back later and watch *Plata* practice his *airs above ground*." He performs them like the horses in the Spanish Riding School do in Vienna. I assure you, he's really quite impressive." A minute later he was running to answer the phone.

Mackenzie was puzzled, "Is that something our Dream can do?"

Her father laughed, "I'm afraid not, Sweetheart. She's good, but it takes a lot of strength in a horse's hindquarters to do those moves. One of those *airs* is called the capriole, which means *the leap of a goat,* because the horse coils his legs under him, jumps straight up into the air, then kicks out with the hind legs, like you've seen goats do. The goal is to land on all four legs at the same time. It requires an enormously powerful stallion to perform this correctly, and is considered the most difficult of all the airs above the ground. Our Dream does not have that strength, but evidently *Sueño de Plata* does."

As they walked back to the house, her father asked, "So what do you think of this place now?"

"It's a dream, Papa. I can see why your father's horses have Dream in their names. It's so perfect here."

Her dad spoke up, "It was very hard for me to leave fifteen years ago, but I loved your mother much more than I loved this place, or these horses ... and I already told you how my father felt at that time. Besides, if I hadn't married your mother. I wouldn't have you, now would I?"

Mackenzie grinned, "Nope. You wouldn't have me."

He reached over and tousled her hair, "Let's go in and see your grandfather. I'm sure he's waiting for us."

Chapter 10

———◌◌◌———

Will Grandpa Perez Visit America?

As soon as he heard the front door open, Grandpa Perez had Maria roll him to the front hall. "So, how did you like my horses?"

Mackenzie answered, "They are beautiful and I'm so glad my foal will have *Sueño de Plata's* bloodlines. He is beautiful!"

Her grandfather answered, "So he is. Did you like the stables as well?"

Mackenzie grinned, "What's not to like? Of course I did. We are redoing our stables in Camden as well, and they're going to be beautiful, too.

"Very nice. Do you have many horses in the stable?"

Mackenzie looked down and muttered, "Not really. Just four, but we have stalls for thirty."

Her grandfather laughed, "Sounds like you need more horses."

She gave him a serious look, "Papa thought we might buy one from you ... to sort of get started. He's been working with Thoroughbreds for many years, but he loves Andalusians best. Iberian Dream has been a great start."

Just then her father came in, "I see you two are getting acquainted. Your granddaughter loves your stable and your horses."

"So she's been telling me."

"She was especially fond of *Sueño de Plata*."

Mackenzie interrupted, "Not just because he's the most beautiful horse I've ever seen, but I will be owning one of his foals when Dream delivers hers in April."

Her grandfather laughed, "He's my favorite as well. Do you think he'd like to live in South Carolina with you?"

Mackenzie looked over at her father, "What does he mean, Papa?"

"He wants to know if you'd like to have Silver come to Dreamland Farm."

She looked shocked, "Do you mean ... do you mean he might come live with us America?"

Her dad answered, "That's the plan. Your grandfather has offered to let us have him for our farm. I think he wants to let America experience our beautiful Andalusian horses, and he thinks we can make it happen."

Mackenzie looked thoughtful, "Yup, I'm sure we can. Camden *is* horse country and some people have been interested in Dream."

Her dad commented, "I guess I'm going to have to finish fixing up Dreamland and set a date for our open house."

Mackenzie was excited, "I'll help, Papa. I can put an ad in the paper and put flyers up around the town."

Miguel added, "And I'll make up a list of horse people I know, and send them a letter. But, I won't mail them to people dealing with Sunrise Farms, because that wouldn't be right." He sounded confident, "I know lots of other horse people though and this will be fun."

Mackenzie smiled, "I *know* it will be fun. Hey, we could put on a show with Silver as the star, but you've got to learn to ride him like Angelo did."

Her dad agreed, "I can't promise anything, but I think I'll get Angelo to teach me what I need to know."

Mackenzie's eyes twinkled, "Or we could invite him over to the opening. He might like seeing where Silver's going to live. I know he'd love to ride and show him off."

He looked down at his daughter, "When did you get so smart? That's a great idea!"

Mackenzie blushed at the compliment, "I just hope he wants to come."

"He will.'

Chapter 11

—∽∾∽—

New Horses for Dreamland

A week later Mackenzie and her father were winging their way back to America, when she asked, "Papa, when do you think Silver will get to America? I can hardly wait."

"Well, it took two weeks last time, so I imagine we have time to finish fixing up the barn and grounds for the grand opening."

She grinned, "Won't Miss Lillian be surprised!"

"She will, indeed."

There was lots of hustle and bustle around Dreamland Farm the next two weeks. Not only were the stalls scrubbed out, but everything broken was repaired, and the sliding doors on each stall were oiled and ready for the horses they expected to arrive after the open house.

At dinner one night, Lillian asked, "Do you have enough feed for the horses, and is the track out back cleaned up and ready? I think the track will be something our horse people will want to see … and use once they bring their horses here. Henry had the starting gate repaired shortly before he died, so I think it's still in working order."

Papa reached over and patted her hand, "Everything is almost ready, Miss Lillian, but thanks for reminding us of things you think might need to be done. Remember, I ran a big Thoroughbred operation at Sunrise for many years, so I know what we need to provide here. I've gotten phone calls from some of the people I contacted, and all seem to be coming. I've set October 1st as the date for our opening. Silver should be here by then, and hopefully, Angelo will ride him."

Mackenzie interrupted, "Miss Lillian, I can hardly wait until you see Angelo ride Silver."

When the phone rang two weeks later, Miguel answered and his face lit up immediately. He covered the mouthpiece with his hand and whispered loudly, "Our shipment is here!" When he hung up, Mackenzie cheered because Silver would soon be in his new home.

Miguel called his friend and borrowed his large horse trailer. When Mackenzie asked him why they didn't just take their two-horse trailer, he said he was trying it out in case they wanted to buy one like it in the future. She shrugged and got in the truck. "Before we pick up Silver, can I go in back and look at the living quarters? You can even sleep out in this trailer."

"Sure you can. Let me know what you think of it because we may be hauling lots of horses in the future."

As before, they waited for their horse to be led through the receiving door. When Silver was led in, Mackenzie was ecstatic, but even more surprised when they led in another horse ... then another, and another.

Confused, she looked over at her father, "Papa, there must be some mistake. I thought only Silver was coming to live with us?"

He laughed as he patted Silver's neck, "Your grandfather and I had a long talk. He thought our new farm needed more horses. He said it was in the best interest of the breed to provide me with quality breeding stock."

"Did he just give you these horses?"

He replied, "Yes, but the gift was conditional. He said I had to keep him up to date on what was going on at Dreamland, and especially with you."

Mackenzie put her hand on her chest, "Me? He wants you to tell him what *I'm* doing?"

"That's right. He doesn't think he has that long to live, so he wants my letters to be full of pictures of you because he's missed so much of your life."

Mackenzie could hardly believe that her grandfather wanted to have a relationship with her after all these years.

"Mac, why is that so hard to understand. He's trying to make up for the time he wasted. He wants to love you the only way he can ... by sharing his horses with us."

Mackenzie petted the horses, feeling their silky coats, and giving them whatever peppermints she had in her pocket.

"Papa, really now, how can you pay for all these horses?"

He took her hands in his and smiled, "I already told you they are gifts from your grandfather. He told me he has many horses, and he wanted to share. You saw all the horses around his stables and in his pastures."

She stuttered, "But why?"

"My brother, Angelo, is inheriting my father's horse farm when he dies, and all the horses but these four. He wanted to give us a wonderful start on our horse farm, so he not only sent us Silver, but another top-quality stallion, and two mares. He said he wanted to make sure their bloodlines did not cross, so there would be no problems breeding them. In fact, the two mares he sent are not in Silver's bloodlines, nor are any of the stallions they've been bred to."

"Why would that make a difference?"

When her dad started to explain Mackenzie tried to interrupt, but he stopped her. "Sweetheart, let me finish. The two mares have been bred to another well-known stallion from another farm, and they are also due to foal next spring. Genetically, it's not good to have half brothers and sisters mate and have foals."

Mackenzie was excited, "Papa, we'll have babies everywhere. It's more than I ever dreamed could happen."

Chapter 12

———*o/o/o*———

Settling In

Miguel made three trips leading the horses into the trailer. He could handle the two mares in one trip, but the stallions tossed their heads, backed up, and did *not* want to be led anywhere. They were tired from the trip, and had an attitude. A young man standing near the trailer helped him, making sure the stallions were loaded safely and not placed in a stall next to each other.

When they were on their way home, Miguel relaxed a little and commented, "I'm so glad the horses were taped up for transit. Who knows what would have happened if they hadn't had their legs wrapped." Occasionally, they heard a thump coming from the trailer behind them. Mackenzie and her dad just looked at each other and smiled, knowing they would be home soon.

When they were almost back to Camden, Mackenzie asked,

"Does Lillian know you are bringing four horses home? I heard you tell her about Silver, but not the other horses."

He laughed, "It'll be a fun surprise for her, won't it? The stable is filling up and will remind her of when she and Henry had lots of horses on their farm."

"Bet they weren't as pretty as these."

"Mac, you are just partial to Andalusians. There are beautiful Thoroughbreds as well."

She smiled, "I know, but these are extra special gorgeous."

"I think so, too, Sweetheart."

When they drove up, Lillian was sitting on the front porch in a rocker. She shouted down to them, "It's about time you two got back. What took you so long?"

Miguel rolled down the window and told her he'd meet her down at the barn. When she got there, he had just unlatched the back of the trailer. She looked confused, "What's all that commotion? One horse can't make all that noise."

"You're right, Lillian. Go sit on the chair in front of the barn and you'll see soon enough." She did as she was told.

Silver was backed out first. The sight of him took Lillian's breath away. "My, oh my, what a gorgeous animal." Miguel immediately led him into a waiting stall. Before she could say more, he backed the second stallion out of the trailer. He was so riled up he dragged Miguel a few feet before he stopped.

Lillian's eyes opened wide, "And who might this be?"

Mackenzie spoke up proudly, "This is Sultan's Dream. Isn't he beautiful?"

She was speechless. Before her was a smoky gray Andalusian

stud. His neck was arched and he held his tail high. Miguel put him in a stall as well, but not next to Silver.

By the time he got the two mares out of the trailer, she was crying with joy. "I didn't expect this, Miguel. These horses are amazingly beautiful. How did you manage to get four horses from Spain?"

He turned to her and shrugged, "I guess my father felt guilty and generous, is all I can say. He wanted us to have a good start here at Dreamland and hoped these horses would ensure great Andalusians will be bred here in South Carolina, as well as in Spain."

Mackenzie spoke up, "The mares are going to foal this spring. Isn't that exciting, Miss Lillian?"

She answered as she wiped tears from her eyes, "It sure is, Little One. My Henry would have been so proud of his farm. He always loved beautiful horses and wanted them to always live here and it's been my dream, too. I was so afraid I'd have to sell to someone who considered horses just a business. I can tell there is love for the animals here, and that's why I sold to your daddy at a price I thought he could afford."

She ran over and gave Lillian a big hug, "We are so glad you did, and we won't disappoint you. Papa's going to breed the best horses this side of Spain."

Lillian nodded in agreement, "I'm sure he will."

Chapter 13

—⟨ง/ง/ง⟩—

Planning the Open House

The horses seemed to be happy at Dreamland. All they really needed was a clean stall, a lush pasture, and someone to bring them feed.

It was now only a matter of weeks before the grand opening, so Miguel put in many hours trying to make everything as perfect as he could before the big day. When friends dropped by to look at the new horses, he stopped and talked with them briefly, which gave him a welcome break.

His best friend, Ned Regan, commented as they looked over the fence at the horses, "How many horses are here now, Miguel?"

He answered proudly, "I have three of Lillian Sweeney's horses, two new stallions, two new mares, plus Iberian Dream, so I guess that makes eight horses."

"And how many stalls are available for boarding?"

Miguel answered immediately, "Twenty-two."

"Do you think you'll be able to fill them?"

Miguel answered confidently, "After our open house, where everyone can see what we offer, I think we can fill most of them. And don't forget, we have three mares foaling in March, which will bring us up to a total of twelve horses. Of course, we won't need three stalls for the little ones until they're older, but I predict in a few years we'll be full."

His friend looked back at the horses, "I will say this, you have the best looking horses around. They maybe not the fastest, but they're certainly impressive."

"Thanks, Ned. That makes me feel like this whole thing will work out. I want to build a great reputation in Camden with these horses."

Ten days until the open house and everyone on the farm was bustling around trying to get the place as perfect possible. Mackenzie shouted over the sound of the lawn mowers, "Papa, don't forget, you must pick up Uncle Angelo at 4:30. I know you don't want to be late."

He poked his head around the corner and grinned at his daughter, "Yes, I know that. You've been reminding me all afternoon. I'll leave early to beat the traffic. By the way, do you want to go with me?"

She put down her pitchfork and wiped her hands on her jeans, "Of course I do, but I have to get cleaned up first. Don't want to greet Uncle Angelo smelling like a horse, not that he would mind."

She ran towards the house to take a quick shower and get dressed. She debated whether to wear a dress or pants to the airport, but she knew her uncle would laugh at her if she wore a dress. He'd never seen her in anything but jeans. She'd save the dress for Sunday and make sure the jeans she put on were clean. He would understand.

When her uncle came down the jetway from the airplane, Mackenzie was surprised, because she'd only seen him in work clothes. She commented, "Boy, Uncle Angelo, you look so handsome. Are you going to dress like that at the open house? Very impressive."

He laughed, "I won't be dressed like this, but I will be in formal riding clothes, to be sure … clothes with a definite Spanish flair. I have to show our beautiful Spanish Andalusian with class."

Mackenzie squealed, "I'm getting more excited all the time. Everyone will love seeing you ride Silver." He smiled as he picked up his luggage and they headed for the truck.

When they arrived at the stable, they went directly to *Sueño de Plata*. The beautiful horse whinnied in recognition, and Angelo murmured to him in Spanish. Mackenzie asked her dad, "What is he saying to him?"

Her dad smiled, "He's telling him how much he loves and misses him." Mackenzie smiled.

Miguel reminded everyone, "Just four days to go." He looked over at his brother and smiled, "Are you willing to help, Angelo?"

He received a smile in return, "Of course. What do you want me to do?"

"Check the fences to make sure they are all in repair, and paint if I've missed a spot. I want this place to be perfect and sparkle."

His brother smiled as he looked around, "All I see is sparkle. You've done a great job here and I know the crowd will be impressed.

Everyone knew much of the work had to be done at the last minute. The stalls had to be mucked out and spread with clean straw, the yard and track out back had to be freshly raked, the grass mowed and trimmed, and of course, the horses had to be groomed until they shone. There were so many things to think about when running a stable like this, especially one of this quality. Miguel knew wealthy horse people were willing to spend a great deal of money for the best accommodations for their horses. They wanted perfection, and he was willing to give it to them. Dreamland Farm was to be a show place, and that's how he wanted it presented at the open house.

Chapter 14

—◈◈◈—

The Big Day

Miguel looked up as his brother pulled out a chair to sit down at the breakfast table, "Angelo, are you nervous? Tomorrow is the big day."

His brother smiled as he poured milk on his cereal, "Not at all. Silver and I have been doing this for years. In fact, that stallion loves showing off what he can do, and this is the perfect opportunity for him to do just that."

Miguel looked down and shook his head, "I wish I could be as calm as you. There is a lot that depends on how our farm is received by the public."

"Miguel, you have nothing to worry about. The farm is beautiful, and everyone is ready. In fact, I bet Mr. Collins, at Sunrise, is having a fit ... and he'll probably have people over here checking you out."

"My goal has never been to make him uncomfortable, but

I confess, I'd like to have some of his clients ... that is, if they believe their horses would do better here."

His brother laughed, "You're giving Sunrise a run for their money, and I think he knows it."

"Yes, he probably does."

Mackenzie skipped into the room and plopped down with her dad and uncle, "Anyone here excited about tomorrow?" They all laughed.'

As she buttered her toast she said, "I think everything looks great. We'll just need to make sure the stalls are cleaned out in the morning, and the horses look their best."

Just then, Miss Lillian walked in the room. "Thank you for sending over a crew to help with the refreshments for tomorrow. Henry and I used to do this every so often and I've missed it." She looked over at Mackenzie, "I'll also be making those cinnamon rolls you and your dad liked so much when you first came out to the farm."

When she left the room Miguel commented, "I don't know where that woman gets her energy. She's always doing something for us."

Angelo spoke up, "I do. She loves having a family and cooking is her way of showing her affection for you."

Miguel nodded, "I think you're right. She's become the grandmother Mackenzie never had, and both of them are loving it."

The day of the open house was brisk and beautiful. The horse farm was spotless and everyone was bustling around to make sure it stayed that way. By ten o'clock there were cars driving in to see what Miguel had done with the old Sweeny farm. They knew it had been great when Henry had owned it, so they wanted to see what changes had been made. The first thing they noticed was the sign over the entrance and the freshly painted white fencing. The barn was still white, but fresh paint made it look brand new.

By ten o'clock there was no parking left on the farm, so many parked on the street outside the fence.

Miguel exclaimed, "Wow! I never thought so many people would attend. We'd better ask Miss Lillian to put her team to work making more food."

Mackenzie smiled, "Papa, it's a nice problem to have. I'm going down by the barn to see if everything is ready for Angelo's demonstration with Silver. Looks like we may have to put on a late afternoon show as well."

He looked over at her, "Have you been giving tours of our farm?"

She replied, "Yes, of course. I'll tell you what everyone is saying after Angelo's second show. I can't imagine anyone would not like our horses. They're so beautiful."

A few minutes later she heard the opening strains of Angelo's music, so she hurried over to the main corral. It was so crowded she almost didn't get a good spot along the fence. When he rode out on *Sueño de Plata*, everyone started talking at once. They had never seen such a beautiful stallion. They were used to the tall, lean Thoroughbreds, but this magnificent horse had his neck arched and his long main and tail flowed as he pranced to the center of the ring.

Miguel stepped up to the microphone, "Ladies and Gentlemen, today you will see steps executed you've never before seen a horse perform. This horse is a beautiful stallion named *Sueño de Plata*, which, in Spanish, means Silver Dream. He is an Andalusian, born and bred in Granada, Spain. In the Middle Ages, Andalusians were the most desired horses in Europe. In fact, they were often presented to kings in other countries to show respect. These horses have exceptional conformation, temperament, and movement. And, as you will see, centuries of breeding for intelligence, bravery, and beauty, are obvious to all who see them. The rider is my brother, Angelo Perez, from Granada, Spain, so initially the music you will you will hear is the 'Theme from Granada'." Miguel motioned towards the center of the ring with a flourish. "I now present Angelo Perez on *Sueño de Plata*, or as you say here in America, Silver Dream."

Angelo urged his horse forward, while Miguel described what the audience was about to see. "First, we will see the *piaffe*. As you can see, Silver is now standing in one spot while performing a cadence trot, almost as if he were running in place. Much of what you see will be found in most dressage routines, but not all, because they require years of training. Also note that not all Andalusian stallions are strong enough to perform what you will see at the end of our demonstration today, but *Sueño de Plata* is exceptional."

The beautiful silver-gray stallion performed beautifully. He executed the *passage*, which was a slow trot where he raised his hooves high above the ground, like he was dancing. Then came the *levade*. Mackenzie heard gasps in the crowd as Silver raised his front legs high off the ground and maintained his position at a 35-degree angle to the floor. She heard people around her saying, "How does he keep his balance that long?" They gasped again as he performed the *curvet*, by making a series of jumps on his hind legs without his forelegs touching the ground.

After Angelo and Silver performed other dressage steps, Miguel interrupted, announcing the highlight of the demonstration. "What you will see next, my friends, is the *capriole*." He laughed, "I'd say don't try this at home, but I'm sure you wouldn't even think about it." The crowd laughed. Just then Silver leapt into the air, drawing his forelegs under its chest. When he reached the highest point of his jump, he kicked out its hind legs, just like a baby goat might when he is excited.

As the crowd went crazy with shouts and clapping, one man turned to his friend, "The only time I ever saw that done was in a documentary on the Spanish Riding School in Vienna. It's even more amazing in person."

When the festivities were over, the crowd left, excited and talking with each other. But, there was one person in the crowd who was NOT pleased. Martin Collins did not trust the opinion of any of his staff to check out the grand opening at Dreamland Farms, so he attended, wearing a hat, sunglasses, and a crumpled raincoat as a disguise. He would see for himself how Miguel's farm was received by the horse community. After Angelo's ride, and the fervor it caused in the crowd, he was not only angry, but scared. The farm might drain off some of his business, especially among his clients who were into dressage. As he drove away he began thinking of ways to make Miguel's farm a failure. No one was going to take business from him, especially someone who had worked for him for years.

When he got home, he called in his new farm manager, "Phil, I was just at Miguel's grand opening and I'm definitely not pleased. I can't tell you what to do to ruin his farm or his reputation, but I want it done … and don't tell me about it. I don't want there to be any connection to me, or to Sunrise." He gave him a sharp look, "Got it? I can't have anything you do traced to me, so you're on your own,"

Phil nodded, "I got it, boss. You can count on me," then he hurried off to get started.

Chapter 15

———⟨ɔɤɔ⟩———

Fire at Dreamland

Mackenzie ran into her father's room, "Papa, wake up! The horses and dogs are going crazy and I think I hear an alarm!"

Within seconds he was on his feet and pulling on his pants. "Mackenzie, call 911. Something must be wrong outside," then he ran out the backdoor towards the barn. Immediately he smelled smoke and thought, "Dear Jesus, don't let it be the horses." The orange glow over the far end of the barn, made him run even faster.

When he reached the barn doors he threw them open to see if anything inside was on fire. Thank God they no longer stored hay above the stalls. That would have been a disaster, but the noise the horses made was deafening. He reached the phone and called the grooms to come help. Horses hated fire, and the smoke inside meant there was fire nearby. His mind raced,

Did I leave anything turned on that I shouldn't have? What could have caused this terrible fire? He could think of nothing except getting the animals to safety. One by one, he and the grooms led the horses out into the fresh air of the pasture, but now he could see the glow of the fire between the boards at the far end of the building. He just prayed the firetrucks would be there soon and put out the blaze. His precious barn was burning and without help he might lose everything ... he knew his horses were okay, but his dreams were turning to ash.

Miguel had already counted the horses and his hired hands before the pumper trucks arrived. He looked back towards the cottage behind his house and could see Miss Lillian on her porch deep in prayer. That's what they needed now. He gathered everyone around and they prayed through their tears.

After the fire had been extinguished, the fire chief approached the group. "Mr. Perez, you are one lucky man. The outside of your barn is badly scorched, but fortunately, only your feed and hay storage area is gone. Do you remember leaving anything turned on in that building that could have started the fire? If our fire marshals find no electrical source for the blaze, I'm afraid we'll have to conclude someone burned your place on purpose. Do you know of anyone who might want to deliberately do this to you or your farm?"

"No Sir, I don't think I have any enemies that would even think of doing something so terrible."

"Well, think about it, and I'll talk with you again when I get the final report." After they shook hands, he departed.

That afternoon Miguel was talking with his brother, when

Angelo asked, "Do you think the owner of the farm you left might do such a thing?"

"Do you mean Sunrise?"

"No, I don't think anyone there would stoop that low."

"Miguel, how much business do you think you will take away from him?"

Miguel thought a minute, "I really don't know. I want to get my name out to get horses boarded here, and I couldn't do that without opening my place up to the horse community. But, I don't think anyone would try to burn me out over a few customers."

The next day the Fire Marshal dropped by the farm, "Mr. Perez, our preliminary investigation showed that the fire you had started in an area where there are no electrical boxes or wiring of any kind, so we have ruled this an arson. I will be by later to get more information from you."

He responded, "I don't know anyone who would do such a thing, but I know my former employer at Sunrise Farms was very unhappy because he was afraid I would take clients away from them. Maybe it was just a random act by some kids in the area."

Mackenzie, who was always full of questions, asked the Fire Marshal, "What do you look for when investigating a fire?"

He looked over at her and smiled, "Determining the cause of a fire is more complicated than it would seem. The first thing we look for is the fire origin, which is normally the area of the most fire damage. We look on the floor level first and if we see a V burn pattern, it's a good indicator a fire may have started there."

Mackenzie interrupted, "What do you mean by a V burn pattern?"

The fireman chuckled, "Fires started at a low point make a V pattern on the wall because fires burn upwards. Sometimes it starts at an electrical box or in the wiring. This fire didn't start near wiring because the wires we found in your building were stiff and melted, so they were damaged by the fire, not by melted copper arcing to a fuse or electric breaker."

She was relentless in wanting to know exactly what happened, "What was used to start the fire then?"

He smiled down at her, "You are sure full of questions today, but they're good ones. After water is drained from the fire scene, accelerants evaporate as a plume and our sniffer dog can find them without us having to dig through the rubble,"

Mackenzie looked at him expectantly, "Well ... did someone start this fire with gasoline."

The Fire Marshal looked over at Miguel, "Yes, it appears this fire was started with gasoline in the hay."

Mackenzie was not done with him yet, "So, do you know where it was set?"

He laughed and looked over at her dad, "She's tough, but yes, we can tell where it was set by where the dogs sniff out the accelerant, or gasoline, on the cement."

He looked up at Miguel and laughed, "Does she ever stop asking questions?" But he continued, "In this case, we have enough clues to determine this fire was set on purpose. You are just lucky you discovered it early, because really intense fires can spread to other structures, like your barn, and all the evidence be destroyed."

He looked down at her again and smiled, "Are we done here? Have I answered all the questions you asked?"

Miguel stepped between his daughter and the Fire Marshal and shook his hand, "Yes, she's done, and thank you for taking the time to give her some answers."

Miss Lillian was waiting in the kitchen when they returned to the house. She spoke up, "The fire was set on purpose, wasn't it?"

"I'm afraid so. I'm not sure how we are going to find out who started it, but I have some ideas."

Later that morning his neighbor called, "I heard the racket when the firetrucks drove up to your house. When I looked outside I could see you had a fire. Are those beautiful horses of yours okay, and do you need any help? I have some extra hay I can bring over."

Miguel had tears in his eyes when he answered, "Yes, Ralph, I'd love to get some hay from you to tide me over. No, the horses weren't hurt, and the horse barn was only scorched. I thank God for that. If I sound a little shaky I'm afraid I'm still in shock."

More calls came in once the word spread that Dreamland had a fire. Soon after, people showed up with food to feed those who wanted to come help clear up the debris and start on the rebuilding. Miguel was amazed at the warmth of his neighbors coming together to help them. Even his church joined in to support the efforts.

Chapter 16

—◦◦◦—

Who Started the Fire?

A day later, Martin Collins, the owner of Sunrise, drove by to see the damage. He hadn't actually told his manager to torch the place, but he knew it had happened. He was not happy to see the bustle of people at the farm. Many were joining in to help Miguel out after the fire. That was not a good sign.

When he returned to Sunrise, he searched until he found the farm manager in the tack room. He couldn't contain himself and shouted, "What were you thinking? You had to know burning their hay and feed building was not going to be enough to stop that farm." He continued in his rant, "Miguel's neighbors, and others who came to his open house last weekend, are there right now helping out. What I really wanted was their horse facility gone." He shouted louder, "Gone … as in horses dead or injured. I didn't just want the horse barn singed. What good would that do? Nothing!" He looked at his manger in disgust, "Phil, you're fired. Pick up your check in an hour."

Phil responded, "But Boss, you didn't say to hurt those horses. I just thought you wanted something done to damage their facility."

"You thought wrong! Now get out of here before I knock you down!"

They didn't know that Jerry, a groom and good friend of Miguel, had been around the corner from the tack room, and heard the men arguing, but didn't want to embarrass them by interrupting. He was shocked by what he heard. He quietly left. That night he thought about the conversation and didn't know whether he should be loyal to his employer, or to Miguel, his friend. The next morning, he slipped over to Miguel's place before going to work.

He found him down near the burned feed shed, still trying to figure out who would set the fire. He quietly approached and tapped him on the shoulder, making Miguel jump. He turned quickly, "Jerry, you can't sneak up on someone like that. You about gave me a heart attack."

"Sorry. I just stopped by to tell you about a conversation I heard at Sunrise yesterday afternoon."

"And? What did you hear ... that they were happy I had a fire?"

He lowered his head and mumbled, "Not exactly. I heard Mr. Collins yelling at Phil ... he's our new farm manager. It sounded like he'd told him he wanted your whole farm gone. He was furious that only a shed was burned. He also said he meant for the fire to burn up your barn *and* your horses."

Miguel grabbed Jerry's shoulders, "Are you sure that's what you heard? I knew he wanted my business to disappear, but the horses as well?" He mumbled under his breath, "I didn't think even Collins could stoop this low."

Jerry looked frightened, "I almost didn't come tell you because I was afraid I'd be fired or worse. That man sounded crazy."

"Would you be willing to tell the Fire Marshal what you told me?"

Jerry squirmed, "Then they'd know I told on them."

Miguel looked him straight in the eyes, "Jerry, you know you did the right thing by telling me, and I know you're afraid of losing your job, but you also know you can come work here if we can get him convicted of arson for ordering someone to burn our place. Please, please consider doing the right thing. You were brave enough to come here, and I'm proud of you for that, but we need the authorities to know about this."

Jerry pleaded, "Why don't you just tell them you heard Sunrise was behind the fire?"

Miguel explained, "They will ask how I know because they can't move forward without either proof or testimony from a witness."

Phil thought for a moment, then dropped his shoulders in resignation, "Okay, okay, I'll do it, but I'm afraid of Mr. Collins and what he'll do to me." He glanced down at his watch, "I better get going so they don't get suspicious. I only told you because you are a good friend, and I thought you needed to know."

Miguel patted him on the shoulder, "I'm proud of you, Jerry. You did the right thing by coming here."

A week later Martin Collins and Phil Nabors were arrested and charged with arson. Not only had Martin been charged, but Phil testified against him to get his charge reduced. He wasn't going to prison alone.

The Carolina horse world was in an uproar. They wanted their horses removed from Sunrise Farms immediately and the natural place to put them was in Miguel's stable, Dreamland Farms.

Mackenzie complained, "The phone has been ringing all week. I don't even have time to get out and ride Dream."

Her dad looked down at her, "Don't complain Mac, this is a good problem to have, but I have to admit there are more people wanting to board their horses here than we have room for."

"What should I tell them?"

"Tell everyone that when Mr. Collins was convicted, the sons put the farm up for sale and it's been sold. Many owners decided to put their horses here and now we're full. From what I've been able to find out, the man who bought Sunrise hasn't been in the horse business long, but he appears to be pretty honest. I guess we can send callers back to them and tell them we don't know much about the guy, but we understand he only boards horses and offers no training. Some I've talked with seem to be comfortable with that explanation."

"Papa, we train as well, right?"

"We sure do Mac, and that's why some horse owners want to come here."

"Thanks for telling me what to say, because I wasn't sure.

I wish we could take *all* the horses in that want to come to Dreamland."

"I know you do, Squirt, but we can't without building another barn and hiring more people."

"And why can't you do that?"

"Think about it, Mackenzie. It would take lots more money than we have, and most of all, we want to keep this a quality facility, not just a barn to board expensive horses. Plus, it's hard to find trainers who really know horses and how to get the most out of them."

She looked up at him, squinting in the bright sunlight, "I agree."

The phone rang again and she scurried to answer it. When she saw it was another caller asking their boarding rates, she looked over at her dad and made a face. It wasn't that she didn't want people to know about Dreamland Farms, but they had no more room and they were turning people away. As much as she wanted to, they could board no more horses.

Chapter 17

—⦿⦿⦿—

Rebuilding Dreamland

While Mackenzie and her dad checked on the horses, she asked a question, "Papa, I'm glad all our stalls are now filled, but what happens when our babies grow up and need a place of their own?"

He turned to her, "Mackenzie, why borrow trouble, because each day has enough trouble of its own."

"You are talking about the Bible again, aren't you, Papa. But here's the way I see it. God doesn't really care if we worry, because it doesn't hurt anyone."

He responded, "You really don't think it hurts you? Worry and stress cause physical problems in our bodies and more than that, it grieves the Lord because it means you aren't trusting him."

She responded immediately, "I trust him, but . . ."

'No buts, Mackenzie. You either trust Him or you don't."

"But ..."

"Think about it. You didn't want your mom to die, but she is now in heaven and happy and healthy. If she were still alive we'd still be on Sunrise instead of being here at Dreamland; we would have never had the opportunity to reconnect with your grandfather and visit Spain, we would not be raising these beautiful Andalusian horses, and we wouldn't have Miss Lillian in our lives."

Mackenzie was quiet and finally said, "So the Bible is right. God works all things out for the good, for those who love him, even if terrible things happen."

"That's right, Punkin'. Now I'm going to tell you something you don't know."

"What's that?"

His eyes twinkled, "You know I filed a claim with our insurance company because our farm was damaged and we needed the money to fix it."

"I already know that, Papa."

"What you don't know is, our insurance companies have been in a mediation to help us compromise so there will be no lawsuit and we won't be going to trial. I tried talking with Mr. Collin's sons when this first happened, but they wouldn't talk to me. In fact, they hung up the phone on me."

"Papa, if they wouldn't listen to you, why aren't you just filing a law suit? Isn't that what people do when someone damages someone else's property?"

"Sweetheart, the Bible strongly discourages law suits against others, especially other Christians, but the sons wouldn't even talk to me, so I've been letting the insurance companies handle it. Now that the insurance companies have worked out a compromise, they've finally taken my call. I told the sons we'd agree to settle for less than the attorneys suggested if they'd give us two fillies they still own. The ones sired by Breakout, their best stallion."

"But Papa, Sunrise was sold to someone else."

He smiled, "But not all the horses were included in that sale. I checked. There are a few left and I've always loved those two. They were yearlings at the time of the fire, which makes them two-year olds now."

Mackenzie was confused, "Papa, didn't I just tell you we have no more room for horses at Dreamland?"

Her father laughed, "But I can build another barn with the settlement money."

Mackenzie's eyes opened wide, "Really! We're going to build another barn?"

He gave laughed, "Yes, we are."

His daughter thought for a moment, "I thought all our new horses were going to be Andalusians?"

"The Andalusian bloodlines are great, but half Andalusian and half Thoroughbred is a great mix for horse people around here to buy, because many are into jumping and dressage. What's not to like? We can breed those fillies to our stallions and come up with some very, very nice horses."

"Papa, why did you suggest such a deal?"

"It could be months, and maybe even years, before a law suit got through the courts. This way we can settle it now and get on with our lives … plus it will give us a couple of very nice fillies."

She asked, "So the horses are coming here for sure?"

He smiled down at her, "I should know by the end of the week if the offer has been accepted, but I believe it will be."

Mackenzie went into her happy dance, "YAY! More horses for us ... and a new barn!"

Miss Lillian heard Mackenzie whooping and hollering before she came in the house. "What's the matter with you girl? You sound like a wild Indian."

"Papa just told me Sunrise may accept our offer and we could be getting two new fillies from them!"

Lillian laughed, "Well, I'd run and whoop it up like you if I was a little younger. I'm just going to smile and congratulate you and your dad."

"Do you know what this means?" She didn't wait for Lillian to answer, "We might get to pick them up soon, and dad will finally be able to tell the contractors to start the new barn!" She gave Miss Lillian a big bear hug and ran back outside to tell the horses ... not that they would understand, but she had to tell someone.

Sure enough, the horses came to live at Dreamland Farms the next week. To her surprise, Dusty, the old hound dog she had always liked at Sunrise, was with them. Mackenzie knelt down and called to him, "Dusty, come her and let me give your neck a hug. Do you remember me?" She gazed into his eyes and talked softly to him as she scratched his neck. "I never thought I'd see you again. Old boy, you're coming to stay with us. I'm so glad Papa remembered how much I liked you, and made you part of the deal. The horses here will love you." She stood up and headed towards the pasture. She was going to introduce the other horses to her favorite dog.

Miguel wasted no time. By the next week there were workers laying the barn's foundation and pulling lumber off the trucks so they could start erecting the barn as soon as the cement dried. Mackenzie asked, "How did you get this organized so quickly?"

He answered, "After the feed shed burned, and we found out who was responsible, our insurance company contacted his and began talks."

Mackenzie was upset, "And you didn't tell me about this plan?"

"You are my little worrier, and I didn't want to add to your concerns."

"Papa, actually that was the kind thing to do because I would have been thinking about it all the time ... and bugging you about it as well."

He gave her a nudge and smiled at her, "I *know* you would have, because that's who you are. You always want to know everything."

She admitted he was right.

The day came when the barn was finished. Mackenzie exclaimed, "You made it look just like the barn Lillian's husband built!"

He looked over at his daughter, "That was my goal. This is such a beautiful place, that I wanted it to blend in perfectly with the buildings already here."

Mackenzie smiled then asked, "When can we start putting horses in the stalls?"

"After you get moving and spreading each one with straw."

"I'm going to go do that right now," and she ran off to find some help, knowing the job would go faster that way.

Chapter 18

—◦◦◦—

New Foals are Born

April came and new Andalusian foals were born. "Papa, come quick! Something's wrong!"

"What is it Mac?"

"The babies are not gray or white like the mares or the stallions."

He started laughing, "I forgot to tell you that grey or white Andalusians are born black, or dark brown, and turn grey or white with age."

"Why?" was all she could think to say.

He answered, "If a white Andalusian is an albino, which means it's born white and its skin is pink, it will stay white. Some horses born with black skin and dark eyes might eventually have a white or gray hair coat. They become lighter each year as the graying process takes place. The fillies we own turned early, but it takes many gray horses six to ten years to turn white."

"How interesting. How come you know all this stuff?"

He laughed, "It could be because I was raised on an Andalusian stud farm."

"Oh, that's right. You're used to dark colts turning gray or white."

They turned their attention to the new foals. One was a male and one was a female, and both were beyond cute to Mackenzie. "Oh, look how they nuzzle their moms, and they get licked."

"Mackenzie, you've been around horses all your life, so you know that's nothing new. That's what horses do. In fact, almost all animals do that."

"I know, Papa, but these are ours and so precious. Hey, Sweet Dream would be a great name for that little girl. Don't you think?"

Her dad looked in the stall, "I can see it fits her. Sweet Dream it is." He moved to the next stall, "Now how about this little guy?"

Mackenzie paused, "It's too early to name him. I want to see how he acts … whether he is shy, happy, or mischievous."

"Mac, you might have to wait several months to find out those things."

"Okay, I get your point. But for now, let's name him Magic Dreamer."

Her dad reminded her, "We can call them whatever we want now, but in a few months, we'll give them their registered name. By then you should know if their names fit."

The new foals grew like crazy. As predicted, Sweet Dream turned out to be a shy little filly, and very sweet. Her name fit, so that's how she would be registered. On the other hand, Magic Dream was not so sweet, and his name did not fit him at all. In fact, the only Dream name that fit him was Bad Dream. He was curious and into everything. He taunted Sweet Dream so much, the filly spent most of her time hiding behind her mother.

Mackenzie turned to her dad, "What are we going to do with him. He's still little, but attacks the other horses in the pasture, then runs to the other end of the field, bucking all the way."

He dad chuckled, "We could name him Spunky Dream because he's so full of energy and seems to irritate the other horses."

"Papa, unless he changes his ways, we're going to have to give him a name that doesn't suit his personality."

"Don't give up, Mackenzie, but try to think up something positive that fits, because I want all my purebreds to be named Dream."

"Dream Racer, because he's always racing around? Dream Hombre?" She paused a minute and laughed, "I know! How about Nightmare?"

"Sweetheart, he's not that bad and I think he'll outgrow his bad behavior. Name him something majestic, because you know he'll be a very fine-looking animal."

"Papa, I want his name to describe his appearance *and* his actions."

Her dad thought a minute then said, "Mac, how about Intrepid Dream?"

She was puzzled, "What on earth does that mean?"

"Intrepid means fearless, bold, and courageous."

She hesitated before answering. "Well, he's those things for sure, and maybe he'll grow into his name and turn out nice. Intrepid doesn't make him sound terrible." Mackenzie slowly said the name out loud, "Intrepid Dream. I like it."

He looked over at her, "There was once a racehorse named Intrepid Lady and her sire was Bold Ruler. He was a famous racehorse in his own right, but he was also the sire of Secretariat, the 9th U.S. Triple Crown Champion American Horse of the Year in 1972–73). I know you know who he was."

She laughed, "What horse person hasn't heard of Secretariat? In fact, I saw a movie about him."

"Mac, one more thing, there was an impressive aircraft carrier named 'Intrepid' that fought in World War II. Fearless was a great way to describe that massive ship." Her dad tousled her hair then headed for the house. He thought, *I'm sure glad to get the names settled. Now Mac can stop calling him 'the colt'. It also means I can register both foals and get the paperwork out of the way.*

Chapter 19

———◦◦◦———

Planning Another Open House

The hot, lazy Carolina summer drifted by, which meant fall was just around the corner. "Papa, when are we going to have another open house at Dreamland? People remember our place as it was last year, before the fire, but now we have a new feed shed and new barn, not to mention more horses. Why don't you call Angelo tonight and see if he'll come again to ride Silver Dream. Everyone loved to see what he could make him do."

"Mackenzie, that sounds like a great idea except we haven't kept Silver in training It would take a while to get him limber and back in shape for that kind of performance."

"So, what's the problem? Angelo loved it here when he visited us, and I know he would be pleased with the changes around here. Besides, he can see Sweet Dream and Intrepid. He's never seen them."

Miguel shook his head, "I know he won't leave dad for that long again. My Papa is old and not well."

She answered immediately, "Have him bring Grandpa. We have plenty of room, and I think he'd like to see the United States, especially Dreamland. He would be so proud of what you've done here. I'd love to see him again, and I know he'd love to see us and America."

"Darlin', he's old and sick, so don't get your hopes up."

Mackenzie pleaded, "At least we can invite him."

When the summer was over, surprisingly, Grandpa felt well enough to make his first trip across the Atlantic Ocean. Though he and Angelo flew first class, and the flight was smooth, they were very tired when they arrived at Dreamland. Miguel showed them to their rooms and told them to rest, but his dad had other ideas.

"Son, I didn't fly all the way across the Atlantic Ocean to sleep. First, I want to see your beautiful Dreamland. Your brother has told me how lovely it is. After the tour I'll lie down for a bit. Angelo has shown me pictures of your babies, but I want to see them for myself."

Miguel smiled at his father, "You are still as stubborn as I remember. Okay, we'll go see the horses, but after that, you must nap so you'll be ready for dinner."

His dad agreed, "A *siesta* then will feel good."

When they got outside, Miguel offered him a wheelchair. In the old days, he would have pushed it away, but he simply smiled and sat down, "Let's go."

As they rolled up to the barn, Miguel's father held up his hand, "*Deténgase, por favor.* Stop, please. I want to look at Dreamland's barn, so I can remember it when I get back to Spain." After a few minutes, he turned to his son, "It's beautiful, Miguel. We can go inside now. After all, I came here to see our babies."

His father responded, "They aren't so young any more. They're already six months old."

His dad smiled, "They'll always be babies to me, like you and Angelo are my babies."

When they heard a neigh from the other end of the barn, Miguel looked down at his father, "Papa, I think they know we're coming to see them."

His father waited while the first one was brought out. He was a prancing, and very energetic, colt. Miguel held the halter tightly, "This naughty boy is Intrepid Dream. In Spanish of course, he is *Soñador Intrépido*. He reminds me of Silver Dream when he was a youngster, because he's full of mischief and energy."

His dad responded, "But don't worry about him, Miguel, Silver turned out to be a magnificent horse."

"That he did, Papa."

"And where is the little filly I've been waiting to see?"

Miguel answered, "I'll be right back with her as soon as I put Intrepid away." A few minutes later he was back leading the beautiful, and surprisingly calm, filly. "This is Sweet Dream and I assure you she's a lady … unlike her half-brother."

His dad looked at her in awe, "She's so delicate looking, but like all Andalusians, she's tough, I can tell that. She's beautiful."

By now he had tears in his eyes. "I can't believe I'm here in America with my wonderful son and his horses. I consider them 'our' horses because they are Spanish through and through."

"Papa, we will have two more foals on the way, but they won't be pure Andalusian. I'll bring the mares out in a minute. I think you'll be pleased."

He looked up at his son, "I know they won't be *Pura Raza Espanola* like Intrepid and Sweet Dream, because they won't be pureblood Andalusians, but let me see the mares. If you picked them out, I'm sure they'll be worthy of our stallion."

A few minutes later Miguel led the two mares out to show his father. He nodded at the first one, a beautiful chestnut, "This is Miss Glory," then he turned to the other, a lovely bay, "And this is Sweet Pearl. Both are registered Thoroughbreds and have excellent bloodlines. They should be very fast."

His dad whistled, "I may not know Thoroughbreds, but I know these two are well bred. And when did you say they're due to drop their foals?"

"In April, which is a little late for Thoroughbreds to give birth, but we wanted to breed them to Silver, so we waited a month or two to breed them."

Miguel's father rolled the wheelchair up close to the mares and reached out his hand to stroke their fine silky coats. "I approve."

When he sighed, they knew he was tired, so they headed back so he could take a quick nap before dinner.

One evening they were sitting the on the veranda together, as they had done many times in the past weeks. The porch fan was gently moving the air, and the ice tea pitcher was close by so they could refill their glasses. His father spoke, "Miguel, now that I see this America of yours I see why you like it. I attended Catholic mass with Angelo last week and it was almost the same as in Spain, except Americans don't seem to dress up as much as we do. If you remember, I also attended your church with you. I expected it to be different from ours, and it was, but it was very nice and I felt comfortable and close to the Lord in there."

Mackenzie asked, "What else about our country is different from Spain?"

He chuckled, "Your hamburgers are different here. In Spain they are made of both beef and pork, then they add sweet or spicy paprika and garlic. And Spaniards have a wonderful French fry dish they call *papas bravas* . We don't use your ketchup, but ours contains lots of our spices, and we even put garlic in our mayonnaise."

"How do you know so much about cooking? I thought you just raised horses?"

He laughed outloud, "Mackenzie, I am a man of many talents and cooking is one of them. I love to cook."

While they were talking, Miguel looked carefully at his father. He actually looked healthier than when he first came to visit. He was sure it wasn't the hamburgers, but being around a family that loved him. Angelo, his other son, had no wife nor children, so there were no grandchildren. Being around his granddaughter had lightened his spirit, and probably improved his health.

Angelo changed the subject, "Tomorrow is Dreamland's

open house. I think the horses are ready to show off. I know Silver is."

Miguel looked over at his dad and his brother, "I'm so glad you both came to see us. It's been a real blessing to have the whole family together. Now Mackenzie knows everyone a little better. She told me she loves you both."

His papa teared up, "I feel so guilty that I pushed you away for so long. I realized in your church service that we truly worship the same God. It's embarrassing to me that it took your wife's death to make me see I needed to make amends. Family needs to be together."

Miguel smiled over at his dad, "What matters is that we are all here today ... and what an exciting day tomorrow will be. If people around here don't already know what Andalusians are, they will by tomorrow afternoon. I've been watching Silver Dream train, and he's in magnificent form. Angelo has done a wonderful job getting him back in shape for the show. I think Silver enjoys it as well, but then, he always was a show off."

Chapter 20

—✥—

Let the Show Begin

Because her grandfather had marveled at the Spanish moss hanging in the trees of South Carolina, Mackenzie Googled it and told him all about it the morning of the open house. "Grandfather, Spanish moss isn't really from Spain, it's native to Mexico, Central America, South America, the U.S., and the Caribbean. Native Americans called it "tree hair." As time went by, they changed the name to Spanish Moss."

He asked, "Mackenzie, how did you get so smart?"

She quipped, "The computer, of course. I often go to the computer when I want to know about something. Being born and raised in South Carolina, I've been around Spanish Moss all my life, but when you asked about it, I became curious."

"You're a smart girl. I think I'll keep you as my granddaughter."

After glancing at the clock, Mackenzie suddenly jumped

up and left the table, then burst in her father room shouting, "Wake up, it's showtime!"

He rolled over and groaned, "Mackenzie, do you have to always be so happy in the morning ... and LOUD? What time is it?"

"Wake up time, Papa! This isn't just any morning, it's our open house, so get your lazy bones out of bed."

"Mac, I'll have you know you aren't the first one to wake me up. The smell of Miss Lillian's cinnamon rolls has been tickling my nose for a few minutes now. She's the one who really woke me up."

"I don't care who woke you up, we need to get going," That's how the day started and continued, with Mackenzie pushing everyone along. She wanted this to be the best open house ever.

The afternoon turned out to be beautiful and many people came to see Dreamland Farms. Mackenzie thought, *aren't they going to be surprised. Dreamland is more beautiful than it was before the fire and there are now more horses now, many of them Andalusians, thanks to Grandpa.*

Mackenzie was excited, but her grandfather was even more excited and proud of the farm. His son had created this beautiful place, and without his help ... well, except for the addition of a few stunning horses. He was very pleased to feel like he was part of his son's success.

When Mackenzie and her grandfather left the house and started for the barn, they were amazed at all the activity. Though she knew everyone had been up before dawn and working to make today wonderful, everyone was bustling around like worker ants. They headed out to check on the horses and found they were restless as well. When she saw her uncle, she shouted over the din, "Angelo, how are the horses doing on this very special morning?"

He shouted back, "As well as can be expected. All I care about right now is getting this day running smoothly and putting on a good performance this afternoon, but I have to admit I'm a little nervous."

"You'll do fine. Just think of the beautiful horse you'll be riding?" He smiled at her then hurried on his way.

Their hard work paid off. The horses were all groomed, and even Intrepid was behaving himself. They were paraded out before the guests, and seemed to be pleased by the reaction of the crowd. Their necks were arched and their coats gleamed, as they pranced, showing off when they heard the cheers. Though Mackenzie's role was simply to lead the horses to the show ring, she was thrilled to be a part of the production. Her dad had done such a great job on this open house and she was proud of him and the farm.

Over the loudspeakers she heard the introduction of her Uncle Angelo and Silver Dream. She pushed her way through the throng of people and found a place at the rail. The music was classical Spanish guitar and so appropriate for what they were about to see. Suddenly, there was a cheer as beautiful horse and rider entered the ring. As a response to the rousing welcome, Silver bowed before the crowd, and from the saddle, Angelo swooped the hat off his head and bowed as well. What a sight they were! Silver's bridle was gorgeous, inlaid with silver and glittered in the sunlight when they moved. The saddle was black and simply styled, but it's buckles were beautiful handcrafted silver. Angelo was dressed in a short black Spanish jacket trimmed with braid and with silver buttons, beautiful riding pants, and highly polished black boots. A black *sombrero-cordobaa* hat sat stylishly on his head. He wore magnificent silver spurs on his boots, but had assured Mackenzie he never used them because they were just for show. He looked stunning and very classy.

The crowd hushed when the music stopped as Miguel picked up the microphone, then looked at his father who was standing behind him. "I want to introduce you to my papa. He may be a little hard to understand because Spanish is his first language, but he can narrate what is about to go on in the ring better than I because he has raised and trained Andalusian horses all his life. He is visiting America for a while, with my brother Angelo. Please give a big hand for my father, Ernesto Perez, from Granada, Spain."

There was a big cheer as Ernesto rose shakily from his wheelchair. "Please pardon my English. Fortunately, I was lucky enough to have many American friends in Spain and have a modest command of your language." He turned to his son, "Thank you my son. Since I'm not sure of my son's routine, I will be glad to tell you what is going on in the ring as it happens. We shall start now, but only after this old man sits down." The crowd clapped.

When the strum of a classical guitar music filled the arena, Angelo and his beautiful horse began moving in time to the music. The crowd was quiet as Silver began to dance and whirl under Angelo's guidance, which was amazing because there was no visible sign he was controlling the horse at all. It was magical.

Mackenzie's grandfather began, "Ahh, now you see the *piaffe*, which is a calm and composed elevated trot in place." He laughed, "Can you imagine your horses doing such a thing? You will see many moves here today that your horses will never do, so I want you to enjoy the performance."

As horse and rider moved to the *passage*, which was a very collected trot, then on to other dressage movements, the crowd clapped and cheered. They really loved the *pirouette*, where Silver turned around on his inside hind leg with the two forefeet and the other hind foot moving around it in the shape of a circle, all in time to the music. The *pirouette* can be performed at a walk and canter. No one could believe this beautiful horse could move like that while still in a canter. Just seconds later Angelo urged the beautiful stallion into a whirling, swirling small circle, while still maintaining his canter. The crowd went wild!

Grandpa Perez was enjoying his role behind the microphone and took the opportunity to give a little history lesson, "As you may remember, these stallions were war horses and ridden into battle by knights, who were, many times, wearing heavy armor. Some believe these moves were originally taught to horses for military purposes because agility was necessary on the battlefield to avoid attackers. However, the movements these Andalusian horses make today would have actually exposed their vulnerable underbellies to the weapons of foot soldiers, so many of the steps you see here this afternoon are simply designed to show the agility and responsiveness of these wonderful animals."

Ten minutes later he announced, "As promised we have

saved best for last. Angelo and Silver are now going to do the *capriole*. Last year my son told you *capriole* 'means leap of a goat,' where the horse starts in a raised position, resting back on his hocks, then jumps straight up in the air, and finally kicks out with his hind legs. He then lands on all four legs at the same time. It requires an enormously powerful horse to perform correctly, and it is considered the most difficult of all the airs above the ground. Watch the horse and rider very carefully, noting the strength you see in his hindquarters. Very few horses, even Andalusians, can do a *capriole*."

Just as Silver was in the raised position, resting on his hocks and coiling for his jump, there was a commotion in the crowd. Someone had thrown a ball into the arena, narrowly missing the horse and rider. There was a gasp and all wondered what would happen now. The magnificent stallion looked at the rolling ball and continued with the *capriole* as if nothing had happened. He leaped into the air then kicked out. Any other horse would have shied in fear and run away from the ball. Not this one. His performance was flawless and nothing was going to break his stride. When he finished his amazing above ground kick, he did another as if to say he was strong and nothing could frighten him. The crowd went wild. They could see this beautiful stallion was not a high-strung horse, bolting at every disturbance. He was calm, collected, and a complete joy to watch.

Many horse owners knew their own horses would have reacted badly. There was something very special about this breed and they thought it might be worth introducing Andalusian bloodlines into their breeding program. Had Mr. Collins been able to read their minds, or overhear their conversations, he would have been furious, but he was now in prison.

Señor Perez was excited, "Ladies and Gentlemen, this is a good example of the wonderful disposition of this breed. They are level headed and don't shy away when confronted with unusual situations. Another reason why I love Andalusians."

As the crowd was leaving, Miguel could hear them talking about his horses and how beautiful and unusual they were. He was pleased. When he turned back to rejoin his father he noticed he was talking with someone. He approached them and excused himself, "Sorry, I hope I'm not interrupting anything." Then he turned to the man, "How did you enjoy the show, Mr. .... sorry, but I did not get your name."

The man smiled, "My name is Keith Bridges and I produce documentaries for a living. I presume you are the son of this very interesting man."

Miguel nodded, "I am his son, and yes, I agree, my father is a very interesting and charming man,"

Mr. Bridges continued, "I find these horses very beautiful and I'd like to tell the world about them in film, so I propose that you and your dad let me follow you around for a few days so we can interview you. We would be filming the interviews, of course."

Miguel wanted to know more. "So, you want to feature our family and Dreamland in a documentary?"

Mr. Bridges smiled, "Not only Dreamland, but we'd like to travel to Spain to film your dad at his horse farm as well. He's been telling me a little about it and it would be a privilege to work with your family."

"This is quite a surprise so we can't give you an answer right now. We must talk about it as a family this evening. I hope you understand."

"Certainly. I'll be in touch with you tomorrow afternoon if that's okay."

"That will be fine."

Later, when they were alone, Miguel turned to his dad, "Well, Papa, what do you think?"

His dad smiled, "It sounds like God is opening yet another opportunity for you, my son, and you deserve it. This will give us something else to talk and pray about tonight at dinner."

Miguel reached for his dad's wheelchair and started pushing it towards the house, "Yes, God certainly works in unusual ways, and I'm not going to argue with him." They both laughed.

Dinner was lively. Not only did they talk about the open house, but about the possibility they would be in a documentary about the family, their horses, and their horse farms. What a blessing to get exposure to the public. The horses would no longer be a secret in America, but the film would show them to be the wonderful animals they are.

When Mr. Bridges called the next afternoon, Miguel told him they would be proud to accept his offer. Dreamland and *Rancho Majestuoso* would be featured, along with the Perez family and their Andalusians. Most of all, it would be a chance for the family to give God the glory for the wonderful blessings they were receiving. They knew he was with them every step of the way and only he could have led them to where to this place.

Epilogue

The documentary aired six months later. Not only was Dreamland overwhelmed with mail and cards, but there were breeders interested in introducing Andalusian blood into their breeding programs. They found the horses unusually beautiful, strong, and even tempered. The family eagerly awaited the first crop of mixed breed foals, to see their strengths and weaknesses in competition.

Sweet Dream was still as sweet and gentle as always, and Intrepid Dream had settled down like his sire before him, into a beautiful horse that loved to show off and please his rider.

The family became closer than ever through what they experienced the past few years, and took every opportunity to praise God for their success. Miguel's father returned to Spain when they shot the documentary at *Rancho Majestuoso*, and was very pleased he now had a video to show his friends when they came over for a visit, so he could brag on his son, Miguel, and show visitors his ranch and horses.

Angelo finally married his long-time girlfriend and they were expecting their first child, which pleased his father very much. Ernesto Perez still loved Mackenzie, but the new grandchild would be a precious bundle he could touch without flying across the Atlantic Ocean to do so. Life was sweet and they all knew Jesus had blessed them all.

Discussion Questions

1. Where in Carolina Dream did someone need to forgive another? In what ways did it change their lives?

2. How has forgiving someone changed your life, if it has?

3. What events happened to make the characters see they needed to trust God? What might have happened if they hadn't? Name times you've trusted God and times you were afraid to trust Him. What happened?

4. When in your life did unexpected good things happened to you? Did you give God the credit? Why or why not? Have you ever blamed Him for bad situations you've faced? Why or why not?

5. What new did you learn about horses in this book? What has encouraged you to find out more about these wonderful animals?

If you enjoyed **CAROLINA DREAM**, you might enjoy
SHADY SPRINGS RANCH
Below is an excerpt:

CHAPTER 1

"Brielle, I want you to realize you're being given another chance to have a normal life with a loving foster family. The Kellingtons are an older couple who lost their daughter three years ago and now they've decided they want to take in and love another child."

There was a long pause with no response. "You can't run away again. Do you understand that? No one wants to take a chance on being responsible for a child who constantly runs away."

Another long pause with no response. "People who take on this responsibility also invest their hearts when they open up to love another child." Vicki Stone shook her head as she watched the wipers swish the rain off her windshield. She wished she could see inside the head of the young girl sitting beside her.

Brielle looked out the window as the car sped towards her new home ... *No, not home*, she thought ... *a new place*. She already knew she'd hate where she was going and would run away again. Maybe next time she wouldn't get found.

When they drove in the driveway, the Kellingtons came out to greet them. They looked like they wanted to run towards the car, but they held each other back and slowed down to a walk. Brielle thought to herself, *how lame.*

She got out of the car and pulled her knapsack from the back seat. She didn't have much, but that meant there would be less to carry when she left. She wondered how long it would be before she grew tired of them and sneaked out of the house late at the night.

She heard, "Hi there, Brielle, welcome to Wimberley, Texas. My name is Brenda Kellington and this is my husband Paul. Welcome to our home. We hope you'll like living here."

Vicki introduced herself to the Kellingtons and followed them up the porch steps. She then turned and looked out over the yard with its many pine trees and well-trimmed bushes, "Lovely place you have here. Brielle has always lived in the city, so this will be a good change for her." Then she turned around and entered the large and inviting log and stone home. She had always loved looking at houses and this one was spectacular.

Brielle admired nothing and said nothing.

Once inside, Brenda turned and offered to get them iced tea and cookies if they were hungry. Vicki accepted the offer, but Brielle simply looked away and flopped down on the closest chair.

It was hard to make conversation with a person who refused to respond, but Vicki continued to talk as if she was getting answers. "Brielle, isn't this a lovely house? It's large and beautifully decorated. I think you'll like it here. I understand it's a working cattle and horse ranch." There was a pause while she tried to think of something else to say, "Weren't those fences we saw on the way in pretty? And, did you notice the horses in the pastures? You might like to go out to their stables later." She finally stopped trying to make conversation and quietly waited for the refreshments to be brought from the kitchen.

After the foster parent contract was signed, Vicki got up to leave. She leaned over and whispered to Brielle, "Remember what I said, this may be your last chance for a placement and the Kellingtons seem to be a lovely couple. Give them and yourself a chance. This could be a wonderful place for you." She straightened up, turned, and walked towards the door, glancing back at the scowling young girl who had moved from the chair and was now sprawled out on the sofa. She silently offered up a prayer, *God, please give the Kellingtons the patience needed to break through Brielle's shell of indifference. Only You can turn this hateful, and probably frightened, young girl into someone loving and special. Help her see these people are being the hands and feet of Christ, offering to show her the way to a wonderful life of peace and contentment. Amen.*

After the door closed, Brenda turned to Brielle and offered her a hand, "Would you like to come upstairs with me to see your room?"

Brielle looked at her new foster mother's hand with disdain, then ignored it as she got up from the couch without help. Brenda simply turned away and said, "Follow me." Brielle followed, but dragged her knapsack behind her, trying to make as much noise possible as they walked up the stairs.

Her room was beautiful. The walls were covered with a light wood paneling and floor was natural stone with thick rugs laid about to take the chill off feet on cold days. It even had an unusual wrought iron screen in front of the stone fireplace. She peered in the large bathroom, but said nothing. She'd never had a bathroom of her own, but she wasn't going to show them she was impressed. Besides, she wasn't going to stay anyway.

The four-poster bed was positioned so she could sit on her bed and look out the window at the Blanco River ... not that it mattered. The beautiful quilt covering her bed was pieced together with muted fabrics and the pillows lining the headboard were fluffed up, soft and full. When her new foster mother left, Brielle sat in a chair by the fireplace and stared into the fire that had been lit to warm her room. She refused to sit on the inviting bed. Tears filled her eyes when she imagined this home and family vanishing like all the others. She always thought she left to avoid being tossed out and wondered how long it would be before she felt rejection again.

A tap on the door jolted her from those thoughts. She responded to the knock in a gruff voice, "What do you want?"

Brenda answered cheerily, "I just wanted to tell you we're eating in thirty minutes so you'll have time for a quick shower."

"I don't want a shower," was the snippy response.

"I'll come back and let you know when we're ready to eat."

"Suit yourself."

Brenda and Paul were making a salad and checking on the chicken roasting in the oven when Paul remarked, "Well, not a wonderful start, but we'll give her time. I just hope she allows herself to get to know us. It would be a shame if she cuts herself off from all the support and love we desperately want to give her."

Upstairs a debate was going on. Brielle was thinking, *should I stay up here and skip dinner to show them I don't care to be around them, or should I go down for dinner, eat, and run back up to my room?* Hunger won out. She could smell dinner cooking and it had been quite a while since she'd had a home cooked meal. Still wearing her old jacket, she slowly made her way downstairs, following the smell of food.

When she rounded the corner into the kitchen she was greeted with, "Hi, glad you could join us." Their cheerful attitude annoyed her, so she didn't respond. She would eat and scoot back upstairs before they started asking her questions. There were always questions. She'd found that out.

As they were eating, Paul commented, "Brielle, you're going to be living here so, if you'd like, you can call us Paul and Brenda instead of Mr. and Mrs. Kellington."

Brielle kept eating and didn't respond, but she was thinking to herself, *why should I call them Paul and Brenda? I'm going to be out of here soon anyway. I don't want them to think I'm getting friendly and fitting into their precious little family. If I keep calling them Mr. and Mrs. Kellington they'll know I'm not going to let them sucker me into caring for them.*

Dinner was surprisingly pleasant. No questions were asked and the only subject discussed was the horses they had on the ranch. As she was getting up to make her break, they asked, "Brielle, since it's still light out, would you like to go down and see the horses?"

She hadn't expected that question. She shrugged her shoulders and said, "Yeh, I guess." The talk of horses at the dinner table had made her curious, because she'd never seen a horse up close. She didn't want to appear too eager, so she hung back as they walked towards the barn.

CHAPTER 2

Brielle could hear the horses before she saw them. Evidently, neighs, snorts, banging, and stomping hooves were common sounds when they were being fed. Very few heads poked out of the stalls at feeding time because they were busy chomping and crunching on their food. It gave her a chance to look in the stalls without some old horse poking his head out, trying to bite her. When she finally peeked in one of the stalls she thought, *oh my, they're huge!* She would have run out of the barn if she hadn't felt protected by a heavy half door between herself and the horse.

Mrs. Kellington looked over at her, "Well, what do you think? Are horses what you expected?"

Brielle shook her head no, then asked, "I know people ride horses, but why would horses let them? They could stomp a person in a heartbeat and kill them."

Brenda answered, "For some reason, horses seem to like people ... at least people that are nice to them. Big dogs could easily slash people with their sharp teeth, but they don't unless they're mistreated. I believe God knew man would need friends, so he made horses and dogs for us to use and enjoy." She chuckled, "Dogs and horses are *very* different from cats. It appears God made man to serve cats." That got a small smile out of Brielle because she *did* have experience with cats.

Brenda then asked, "Would you like for me to take this horse out so you can get a better look?"

Brielle backed up and stammered, "No, that's okay. I can see it from here."

When she got back to her room she thought about the horses and how big they were. Brenda had petted each horse and none had tried to bite her. In fact, when she gave them each a slice of apple, they didn't lunge and grab it from her. They simply nibbled with their lips and gently lifted it from the palm of her hand. Maybe there was something to God making horses to serve man. She knew most dogs were like that, too. They loved people to pet them unless they'd been abused and taught to hate. She would have to think about that. Then she began to wonder if people were also like that ... rejecting people because they had been rejected ... or because they expected to be rejected.

The Kellingtons saw very little of Brielle over the next few days. She ate with them, but stayed in her room the rest of the time, curled up in a wingback chair by the fireplace, reading the many books she found there. She thought this may have been their daughter's room and these were her books. She must have loved to read, too.

Occasionally, Brenda knocked on the door and peeked in, gratified to find Brielle with her nose in a book. *Good,* she thought, *she loves to read like my Tammy.* Those thoughts always brought a tear or two because she had many good memories of her daughter.

When Brielle had exhausted the supply of books in her room, she asked Mrs. Kellington if she could look in the downstairs library for more. She was told she could. When she left the library, she was asked who had taught her to love reading.

That was another question she hadn't expected, so she answered without thinking, "My mom loved to read before she started doing drugs. She would say it was a way to take a trip without leaving the farm." Brielle was afraid there would be more questions so she quickly scurried upstairs and shut the door. Had she said too much? Why had she shared that her mother was a drug addict? She could have kicked herself. Giving out that kind of information would certainly bring more questions and she hated questions.

A week later Brielle was awakened by noise in the driveway. She looked out her window and saw Mr. Kellington talking to a man who had just driven in pulling a horse trailer. He motioned for the man to drive over to the barn and told him to wait for him there. Mrs. Kellington joined him and they both trudged after the trailer. Brielle was curious and wondered what she was missing. She quickly threw on her clothes and joined the procession. When she got close to the barn, she hid behind a bush so she could see what was going on without them seeing her. It wouldn't be good to let them know she was curious about something going on at the ranch.

Mr. Kellington called out, "Mac, let the ramp down slowly and back her out. We don't want to scare her any more than she is already." A very scraggly, reddish-brown horse was backed down the ramp into the yard. It didn't look *anything* like the other horses here on the ranch. This one was very skinny, with a matted coat, and looked exhausted.

Mrs. Kellington took the lead rope and went to the horse's head, giving her a pat, "It's okay, girl. Things will be better now." The horse nuzzled her and nickered softly.

Brielle wondered, *why was that old horse brought here?* When her curiosity got the better of her, she stepped out from behind the bush. "Good morning. I heard someone pull up and saw everyone heading towards the barn. What's happening?"

Everyone looked up at the sound of her voice, surprised she was out of bed since it was only seven o'clock in the morning.

CPSIA information can be obtained
at www.ICGtesting.com
Printed in the USA
FSHW021827260519
58451FS